Mrs. Pollifax opened her eyes
to find that a cold wind had sprung up and was blowing through the door to the balcony, presenting her with the choice of getting up and closing the door or getting up to look for a blanket. Neither prospect appealed; she wanted only to sleep. As she lay and rebelliously considered these alternatives, a curious thought occurred to her: she had not left the balcony door open. She had closed and locked it.

A moment later she realized that not only was the door open but that someone else was in her room with her.

A Palm For
Mrs. Pollifax

by Dorothy Gilman

FAWCETT CREST • NEW YORK

palm: a leaf of the palm as a symbol of victory or rejoicing.

Selection of the Detective Book Club,
September/October 1973
Selection of the Readers Digest Condensed Books,
Spring 1973

ISBN 0-449-23446-0

Printed in the United States of America

First Fawcett Crest Edition: September 1974

20 19 18 17 16 15 14 13 12

One

It was morning and Mrs. Pollifax was seated on the floor of her living room, legs crossed beneath her as she tried to sustain the lotus position. She had been practising Yoga for a number of months now. She could almost touch her forehead to her knee, she could roll over backward into a ball, and once—propped up by Miss Hartshorne—she had stood dizzyingly on her head. But she could not manage the lotus position for more than a minute and she had begun to despair of becoming a Contemplative.

"I'm too cushiony, I can't fold," she sighed, and rued the more than sixty years in which she had sat on chairs, couches, stools, and pillows but never on the floor. At the moment this mattered a great deal to her but the moment passed. It was, after all, a delightful and sunny day, there was work to do and at noon a meeting of the Save-Our-Environment Committee. As she climbed to her feet she heard Miss Hartshorne calling her name from the hall, and a moment later her neighbor in 4-C reinforced the summons with a loud knock on the door.

Mrs. Pollifax padded across the room in her leotards. It was only 9:15 but the middle of the day for Miss Hartshorne, who took brisk walks at six, and Miss Hartshorne's energy could be devitalizing. Mrs. Pollifax braced herself.

But her neighbor was not disposed to linger this morning. "I was just leaving the building," she cried breathlessly, "when a special delivery came for you, Emily, and knowing you probably aren't even *dressed* yet"—here her voice wavered between disapproval and tolerance of a friend's eccentricities—"I took the liberty of signing for it."

"Kindness itself," said Mrs. Pollifax cheerfully. "Going shopping?"

"Oh dear no," said Miss Hartshorne, shocked. "It's Tuesday." And presenting Mrs. Pollifax with the letter she hurried away.

"Tuesday," repeated Mrs. Pollifax blankly, but having no idea what that meant she turned her attention to the letter. It was postmarked Baltimore, Maryland, and she wondered who on earth she knew in Baltimore who would send a letter both airmail and special delivery. It implied a distinct note of urgency. Baltimore . . . urgency . . . At once Mrs. Pollifax found herself recalling certain small, secret trips she had made in the past for a gentleman named Carstairs, and the cover address in Baltimore that she had twice been given. She felt a catch of excitement. Closing the door she slid a finger under the flap of the envelope and drew out a sheet of paper emblazoned with the letterhead of one William H. Carstairs, Attorney-at-Law, The Legal Building, Baltimore, Maryland.

"Attorney-at-law indeed!" she sniffed, and sat down. "What on earth—!" The letter appeared to be a carbon copy of the original but the address to which it had been sent was carefully deleted. Across the bottom of the page, in red pencil, Carstairs's assistant had scribbled, *We need you, what are you doing on Thursday?*

Mrs. Pollifax began to read the letter:

Dear M. Royan, it began. *In reply to our telephone conversation of this morning I am enclosing the suggested deposit of five hundred dollars for the convalescence of my mother-in-law, Mrs. Emily Pollifax . . .*

"Mother-in-law!" said Mrs. Pollifax in a startled voice. "Convalescence?"

. . . at your Hotel-Clinic Montbrison. It is of the utmost urgency that she be given rest and treatment . . .

The telephone began to ring and Mrs. Pollifax edged toward it, her eyes on the letter. Plucking the receiver from its cradle she said, "Yes, yes, I'm here," in an absent voice *. . . and I shall persuade her to place herself entirely in your hands. I am delighted to hear . . .*

"Mrs. Pollifax?"

"Speaking, yes." *. . . that room 113 will be reserved for her with its private bath and view of the lake . . .*

"Mr. Carstairs's office calling, will you hold, please?"

"Oh, gladly," she cried in relief and put down the letter, thoroughly alert now, her heart beating rapidly because both letter and telephone call meant that her life was about to accelerate again, adjust to that fine edge of danger which—like eating fish riddled with small bones— exacted the most scrupulous awareness in order to survive.

The next voice on the phone belonged, not to Carstairs, but to Bishop, his assistant. "He's already left for the airport," Bishop told her. "He's hoping you can meet him in New York at twelve o'clock noon at the Hotel Taft. If you can't manage this I'm to intercept him at the airport, but since it takes so damn long to get to the airport these days—"

"It's that important?" breathed Mrs. Pollifax.

Bishop sighed. "Isn't it always?"

"I have this letter, it just arrived and I was reading it."

"Damn, it should have arrived yesterday," said Bishop. "I insisted Carstairs give you some advance notice this time. Well, hang onto it, that's clue number one for you. I haven't asked how you are yet, Mrs. Pollifax, but I will as soon as I hear whether you can possibly get to New York this morning."

"Yes, I can. Let me think," she said. "It's just 9:45 here—"

"Here, too," put in Bishop helpfully.

"And there's a train at—I can be there by noon, yes," she said. "*If* I hurry."

"Then I won't ask how you are," Bishop said frankly. "You're to go directly to room 321 at the Taft, have you got that? Don't stop at the desk to ask, we'd rather you didn't. I hope to hell your telephone isn't tapped."

Mrs. Pollifax said in a shocked voice, "Why ever should it be?"

"God knows. Have you joined anything lately?"

"Only the Save-Our-Environment Committee."

"Bad," he said gloomily. "Room 321," he repeated and hung up.

"Well," thought Mrs. Pollifax, "I daresay whatever Mr. Carstairs has in mind helps save the environment, too. Loosely speaking," she added, and hurried into the bedroom to exchange leotards for a suit. "Wrinkled," she noted crossly as she glimpsed herself in the mirror, and sighed over the multiplying hobbies—environment, karate, Garden Club, Yoga, a little spying now and then—that left her so little time for grooming. She solved the immediate problem by jamming her newest hat over her flyaway white hair, telephoned for a taxi and several minutes later was descending by elevator to the front door of the Hemlock Arms.

At 11:58 Mrs. Pollifax stepped out of the elevator at the third floor of the Hotel Taft and walked down a carpeted hall. The door of room 321 stood wide open, and for just the briefest of moments Mrs. Pollifax entertained thoughts of skulduggery, of Carstairs lying inside in a pool of blood, perhaps, and then a white-jacketed waiter backed into view; behind him stood Carstairs, tall, leaner than ever and very much alive.

"Hello there," he said, glancing up, and after tipping the waiter he shook hands warmly with her. "I ordered coffee and sandwiches—it *is* good of you to hurry. Come inside so we can talk."

"You've grown sideburns!"

"One must move with the times," he said modestly, closing the door behind them. He turned and studied her with equal frankness. "You look splendid. As a matter of fact much too healthy for what we want. White powder," he mused. "A cane perhaps?" He shook his head over her hat. "Wild. Sit down and have some coffee."

Mrs. Pollifax sat down and he wheeled the cart toward her, pouring coffee for them both,

"Bishop says you received a copy of the letter?"

"This morning." she acknowledged. "Something about becoming your mother-in-law and convalescing from some nameless disease but no hint as to where the letter or I would be going."

"Exactly," he said. "The sandwiches, by the way, are bacon, lettuce, and tomato." He seated himself nearby, coffee cup in one hand. "That letter was supposed to have reached you yesterday, damn it. Because *if* you can do this job for us you'll have to leave day after tomorrow, on Thursday."

"If?" she inquired with a lift of an eyebrow.

"Yes." He hesitated. "We need you but I have to warn you this assignment is different from the others. It's not a courier job."

Mrs. Pollifax put down her sandwich and looked at him. "I'm being promoted!"

He laughed. "Promoted to new hazards is more like it. Mrs. Pollifax, I have to ask if you're still open to these insane games of Russian roulette or if your sentiments on that score have changed."

"You mean the dangers," she said, nodding. "But of course it isn't at all like Russian roulette," she added earnestly. "Not at all. I always enjoy myself so much—quite selfishly, I can assure you—and meet the most astonishing people. In any case it's difficult to look ahead, isn't it? I can only look back to previous trips, in which there were a number of risks—"

"To put it mildly," agreed Carstairs.

"—but they never seemed excessive at the time, or less than worthwhile. No, my sentiments haven't changed, Mr. Carstairs."

"Thank God," he murmured, and then with a snap of his fingers, "I forgot Bishop!" Jumping to his feet he hurried to the telephone and Mrs. Pollifax saw that during their conversation the receiver had been removed from its cradle and propped against the lamp. Picking up the receiver Carstairs said, "You heard, Bishop? Call Schoenbeck in Geneva and set things in motion. Have him deliver my letter within the hour and remind him to double-check those postal markings." He hung up. "Now you know where you're going. Switzerland."

She brightened. "Oh, how nice! I did hope I wasn't going behind the iron curtain again. After being expelled from Bulgaria—"

He grinned. "Well, it's not every member of the New Brunswick Garden Club who can be expelled from Bulgaria, is it? Ushered to the airport and told to get out and stay out, forcibly and irrevocably. Let's see what you can do with Switzerland. I want to place you in the Hotel-Clinic Montbrison as a patient, but while you're there under medical observation, so to speak, you will in turn please observe the Clinic."

"Is it a clinic *or* a hotel?" asked Mrs. Pollifax, puzzled.

"We're not accustomed to the combination in America," he admitted, "but European habits differ. Montbrison is a medical clinic to which the wealthy of the world repair for treatment, to rest, convalesce, lose weight, that sort of thing. The hotel concept makes it all palatable and exceedingly pleasant and I'm told the food is superb. It has a considerable reputation internationally, drawing people from the Middle East as well as Europe."

"But you're not sending me there to rest," she said tactfully.

Carstairs shook his head. "No indeed." Returning to his

chair he sank into its depths to ponder her over steepled fingers. "We're in trouble, Mrs. Pollifax," he said at last bluntly. "I can't tell you all the facts, it's classified information and since it now involves Interpol it's not my story to tell. To wrap it up in one sentence, however, there have lately been two small, very alarming thefts of plutonium, the first one here in America, the more recent in England."

"Plutonium!" echoed Mrs. Pollifax. "But that's used in—"

"Exactly. The stolen pounds add up to a dangerous amount when put together—almost enough, in fact, to make a small atom bomb. Plutonium is man-made, you know, it's processed in a nuclear reactor. This has kept it a toy of the moneyed countries and completely inaccessible to any underdeveloped countries—or was," he added savagely. "The two thefts took place within the same month and with uncanny efficiency. We think they're related. We've no idea who's behind them but we've reason to believe that one of the shipments was sent by mail to the Hotel-Clinic Montbrison."

"Can something like that be sent through the *mail?*" said Mrs. Pollifax incredulously.

"Oh yes. To make that one small atom bomb, for instance, you need only eleven pounds of plutonium. Which is what terrifies us," he added pointedly. "So far nine pounds are missing, and if you've managed a package of that weight you know it's relatively light, you could carry it easily in a suitcase. Damnable business, as you can see." He moved to a leather case on the table and drew out a slide projector. Wheeling the table to the center of the room he said, "Mind turning off the switch just behind you?"

With the room in twilight he turned on the projector and a square of white light appeared on the opposite wall. A moment later it was occupied by a close-up of a small wooden crate. "This is how we think the shipment looked," said Carstairs, "or so we've deduced from the information we have. Black letters stenciled on each side of the box saying *MEDICAL—HANDLE WITH CARE.* On the top, stenciled in red the words *MEDICAL SUPPLIES—FRAGILE.*"

"That's not the actual box?"

Carstairs shook his head. "A reconstruction from a description given us, but how accurate it is we don't know. It's believed to have been shipped *Airmail-Special Delivery-Special Handling.* It would have been delivered to the Clinic—unless it was intercepted on the way—nine days ago."

"Would it still be there?" asked Mrs. Pollifax in surprise.

"We can't be sure. Interpol put one of their men into the Clinic as a waiter, with the co-operation of the Swiss police. This man—his name is Marcel, by the way, and he's still there—found no traces on the premises. After his search produced nothing the British sent one of their Intelligence people in as a patient, a man named Fraser." He hesitated and then said quietly, "Unfortunately Fraser had an accident, Mrs. Pollifax. There's no possible way of describing it without sounding ridiculous but two days ago Fraser fell off the mountain near the Clinic. He was dead when they brought him out of the ravine."

"Oh dear," said Mrs. Pollifax. "Under the circumstances, it sounds more suspicious than ridiculous, don't you think?"

He nodded grimly. "We thought so, yes. We'd nearly crossed the Clinic off our list when that happened but Fraser's death made it a whole new ball game." He frowned. "I should add that we've not been completely frank with the people at the Clinic."

"Oh?"

"They've been told it's hard drugs that we're investigating, and that some kind of surveillance would be set up. They asked only that we be discreet, which is quite understandable, but we've not taken them into our confidence about Fraser or Marcel. We won't about your presence, either." He added dryly: "After all, it could be someone closely connected with the Clinic who's using the place for illegal activities."

"So they don't know."

"They don't know, and now Fraser's dead. It could have been a freak accident or he could have stumbled onto something. In that case—" He tactfully refrained from completing the sentence and said instead, "You have me to blame, Mrs. Pollifax, for recommending you and volunteering your services. The Swiss are co-operating in every way they can. Interpol is, of course, heavily involved, as well as the American government—and therefore my department—and the English have a stake in this, too."

The compliment was unspoken but obvious; Mrs. Pollifax leaned forward and said doubtfully, "But do you really think that I—?"

He threw up his hands. "I can think of at least ten agents of mine who are well-trained, experienced and Gung Ho, and I'm sure the English can, too." He frowned. "But aside from your record, which is startling, I have a feeling that this situation needs something more than training and experience. It needs a rare kind of intuitiveness, a talent for sniffing out what others miss. You're rather good with people and you simply don't act or react like a professional agent." He added abruptly: "What we are looking for—aside from stolen plutonium, Mrs. Pollifax—is evil in its purest form."

"Evil," she mused. "That's an old-fashioned word."

"Positively Biblical," he agreed, "but you have to remember that stolen plutonium is not quite the same as stolen money, Mrs. Pollifax. The uses to which illicit plutonium can be put are very limited but one of its uses is hideous to contemplate."

"Hideous," she said, nodding.

He leaned over his slides again. "I think you'd better

see what was inside that crate. It's quite unlikely you'll discover any of these items sitting about on someone's desk as a paperweight but one never knows. Here we are —exhibit number one."

Mrs. Pollifax studied the innocent-looking object projected on the wall. *"That's* plutonium?"

"Yes, shaped into a metal button weighing about two kilograms. Not very prepossessing, is it?" He switched to another slide. "Each button was then individually packed into a plastic bag—there's your plastic bag—and then," he added, changing slides, "the bag was placed in a can filled with inert gas, which in turn was placed inside this odd-looking contraption they call a birdcage, probably because—"

"Because it looks like a birdcage," finished Mrs. Pollifax.

"Yes. Five pounds of plutonium were in the crate stolen from England. If you come across any of these items, don't touch. If you have to touch, use surgeon's gloves." He shook his head. *"If* you find anything. *If* it's there. *If* more should be sent. If, if, if." He sighed and returned to the projector. "Now I want to show you a diagram of the Hotel-Clinic Montbrison before we conclude this. You recall it's room 113 that's been reserved for you."

"Any special reason?"

"Oh, yes. From the balcony of room 113 you'll have a marvelous view of Lake Geneva. You will also be able to see from your balcony, on your left, a narrow, very primitive dirt road, incredibly steep, that winds and circles up the next mountain. From any other floor it's screened by the trees." He flicked on a new slide, a larger diagram that showed the terrain surrounding the Clinic. Standing up he pointed to a small X. "There's your road, off on this mountain here. Every night at ten o'clock—it's quite dark by then—there'll be a car parked at a point on the road that you can see from your room. You'll signal from your balcony with a flashlight. That will be your contact with the outside world."

She frowned. "Won't anyone else see me signaling?"

He shook his head. "Room 113 is quite high. Actually it's on the third floor because the Clinic's built into the mountainside. The massage and treatment rooms are on the ground level, the reception and dining rooms are on the next level, and the patients' rooms begin above that. As soon as you've signaled each evening the car will turn on its lights—you'll be able to see that—and proceed down the hill. You'll flash your light twice if all's well but if you've something urgent to report you'll blink your light four times."

"And what will happen then?" she asked with interest.

"Then you can expect an incoming phone call within the half hour. Since it will come through the Clinic's switchboard we'll work out some kind of simple code for you, based on your health." He unplugged the projector and carried it back to its case. "Other than this," he said, "your job will be to mingle with the guests, do as much judicious exploring of the building as possible, watch, eavesdrop, listen, and don't admire any sunrises at the edge of a one-hundred-foot drop."

"I won't," she promised.

"We've booked you for a flight to Geneva on Thursday —the day after tomorrow. The letter confirming your arrival at the Clinic will be received by them today, and tomorrow I'll cable them the hour of your arrival and ask that you be met at the airport by a limousine, as befits the mother-in-law of a noted Baltimore lawyer," he added with a grin.

"And what am I recovering from?" asked Mrs. Pollifax.

"If you've nothing more exotic in mind, how about a stubborn case of good old Hong Kong flu?"

"All right," she agreed, "but what equally concerns me if I'm leaving so soon is what I tell people when I announce I shall be away. People like my son in Chicago, my daughter in Arizona. The Garden Club. My neighbor Miss Hartshorne, the Art Association—"

"Go on," said Carstairs, looking fascinated.

"—the Hospital Auxiliary, the Save-Our-Environment Committee and"—she paused to frown at the expression on his face—"my karate instructor."

"I waited for the last with bated breath," Carstairs said. "It still carries impact."

"My karate strikes do, too," she told him modestly. "But what is my New Brunswick—" She searched for the proper word. "Cover."

"Ah yes. Well, at short notice the easiest is the best, I think. I suggest you visit an old friend named Adelaide Carstairs living in Baltimore. If any calls come through for Adelaide they'll be diverted to my office." He grinned. "I'll leave it up to you to embroider on Adelaide, I'm sure you can come up with something dramatic."

He glanced at his watch. "Good Lord, one o'clock! Have I covered everything? Damned nuisance not having Bishop with me, I'll have to spend the next hour making arrangements for your departure."

"On Thursday," she reminded him.

"Right, at 6 P.M. but I want you at Kennedy International by four o'clock. You'll be paged over the loudspeaker system and given another briefing, as well as your tickets and the code that we'll establish for you. I'd rather not have you paged under your own name. Can you suggest one?"

"Jones, Johnson, Smith," she said quickly.

"We'll make it Johnson. Mrs. Virgil Johnson." Rising he held out his hand to her. "Well, Mrs. Pollifax," he said with a rueful smile, "here we go again."

"Yes," she said, rising and shaking his hand.

"Bon voyage. Finish your bacon, tomato, and lettuce and leave the key at the desk downstairs." At the door he stopped with one hand on the knob. "And damn it, don't disappoint me by getting your head bashed in."

She was really quite touched by the emotion in his voice. She returned to her sandwich wondering whether Adelaide Carstairs should be an elderly aunt who had broken her hip—rather dull, that; a niece who had eloped with a scoundrel, or a friend who had just been swindled and desperately needed comfort and advice.

She would have been swindled, decided Mrs. Pollifax, by a tall man with a scar over his left eyebrow. He might have a slight limp, too—that always aroused maternal feelings—but he would definitely be very distinguished and have impeccable credentials.

In the end Mrs. Pollifax sadly dispensed with her distinguished swindler and turned Adelaide Carstairs into a plain old school friend, recently widowed.

I'm sure you remember my speaking of her, Mrs. Pollifax wrote her daughter in Arizona that evening. Of course Jane would not remember her, but since children paid very little attention to their parents' friends Jane would probably reply that of course she recalled Adelaide Carstairs. *I'll just go down for a week or two and cheer her up,* she added, giving the Baltimore address in case of emergency, but after sealing the letter Mrs. Pollifax sat and stared at her desk blotter without seeing it for a few minutes. She was thinking of her grandchildren and the vocabulary that had been devised for the world into which they'd been born, words that were as familiar as cat and dog to them: megaton and isotope, military-industrial complex, nuclear capability, ABM, MIRV, arms race, defoliants, and at the end of that list DNA, the genetic material that one reckless person could distort forever with a small bomb containing eleven pounds of plutonium.

Madness, she thought with a shudder.

The next morning, feeling more cheerful, she walked

downtown to do a little shopping, but with no intention of buying either a dowdy hat or a cane; she had in mind a dinner dress. For a long time Mrs. Pollifax had nursed a secret longing to buy something more contemporary than offered by the third floor matrons' department. She headed for the Psychedelic Den and spent a very interesting hour chatting with a young clerk in mini-dress and boots who labored under the impression that Mrs. Pollifax was going to a masquerade party. "Which, in a way, is quite true," she thought.

What she brought home was a long purple robe and an assortment of prayer beads. The robe made her look rather like a fortune-teller or the high priestess of a religious cult but it was a satisfying change. It was also drip-dry, she reminded herself virtuously.

Next it was important to explain her departure to Miss Hartshorne, and this required tact. "She's feeling lonely," Mrs. Pollifax told her neighbor over a cup of tea. "Period of adjustment, you know." By this time Adelaide had taken on shape and substance and she was finding it difficult to remember that Adelaide did not exist. "She and her husband were very close," she added.

Miss Hartshorne's mouth tightened. "I think I've been your friend long enough to say what I think of this, Emily, and I don't think much of it at all. You leave New Brunswick only when a sick daughter-in-law or a friend sends out an S.O.S. and I must say these calls for help have been increasing lately. You let people take advantage of you."

"Grace, I'm quite happy to—"

"I've tried for years to persuade you to do some traveling with me but no, you simply won't travel at all. What you lead, Emily, is an unhealthily dull life."

"Yes," said Mrs. Pollifax meekly.

"You know that ever since my retirement I've taken one Cook's tour a year—religiously—and if I may say so, Emily, it's what keeps me young. You never go anywhere interesting, you never meet new people, now do you?"

"Well," began Mrs. Pollifax, taking a deep breath, but Miss Hartshorne was not waiting for a reply.

"It's no vacation at all, cheering up an old friend, and don't think I haven't noticed how tired you are when you return from these little trips. Your essential problem, Emily, is that you have no sense of adventure."

"None at all," said Mrs. Pollifax, beaming at her friend, "but won't you have another cup of tea, anyway, Grace?"

Two

*"Your attention, please . . . your atten-*tion, please . . ."

Mrs. Pollifax glanced up from her thoughts, which had been occupied by the people hurrying past her intent on carrying babies, cameras, back-packs, luggage, attaché cases, odd packages, and nameless hopes. She had been thinking that her own plans were small and tentative: she hoped to find several pounds of plutonium.

". . . will Mrs. Virgil Johnson go to the Information Desk . . . Mrs. Virgil Johnson . . ."

Obligingly Mrs. Pollifax picked up her suitcase and carried it across the aisle to the Information Desk. Almost at once a man detached himself from the crowd and hurried toward her carrying a suitcase in one hand and a bouquet of flowers in the other. She peered at him in astonishment. *"Bishop?"*

He leaned over and kissed her lightly on the cheek. "In the flesh, isn't it amazing?" He thrust the flowers into her hand. "Beware the Greeks bearing gifts. How are you? I'm delighted to see you."

"And I you," she said, beaming at him. "It never occurred to me they'd send—that is—"

"Ssh, Mrs. Johnson," he said conspiratorially, and picked up her suitcase. "Follow me." He led her around the corner to a door marked PRIVATE. PERSONNEL ONLY. Opening the door he ushered her in and locked the door behind them. "We're being loaned this office for ten minutes. Displaced Personnel is—are?—having a coffee break."

"Are, surely?" she suggested, frowning.

He shook his head. "Is, I think. Oh, grammar be damned, they're gone anyway." He placed his suitcase on the desk. "You realize you're giving me a disastrous time of it by taking on this job, don't you? Carstairs can't make up his mind whether he's sending you up a blind alley or into a lion's den. Today it's a lion's den and he's in a dither."

"Oh, but he appeared *quite* calm about it all when I saw him," she told him. "Really, everything sounds very simple."

"It does?" Bishop looked startled.

"Yes, and it will be such a pleasant change for me, staying in one place."

"I see." He sounded amused. "Well, then, let's get on with it, shall we?" He opened his suitcase. "My bag of tricks," he explained. "I have here for you one flashlight of unparalleled quality." He handed it to her. "Plus a supply of spare batteries in case the quality is not unparalleled —we can't risk a communications breakdown."

"Flashlight and batteries," repeated Mrs. Pollifax, opening her own suitcase and tucking both inside.

"One code in a sealed envelope that also contains rather a lot of money in Swiss francs. The code you will kindly memorize en route and then very thoroughly destroy. One pack of matches with which to destroy said code—"

"You think of everything," she told him admiringly.

"Of course," he said blithely. "And—oh, you are going to have a fun time!—one Geiger counter."

"Geiger counter!" She was startled. "Carstairs didn't mention a Geiger counter."

"Actually a scintillator counter," he amended, pulling out a handsome leather box. "He left it for me to mention because when he saw you we were still working out how to conceal it. You simply can't go poking about for radioactive stuff without some help, can you? Take a look at this." He opened the box.

"Jewels!" she gasped. "Are they real?" She was staring at a flannel-lined tray in which nested an emerald pendant, an enormous diamond pin and two necklaces glittering with rubies.

"I'm sorry to tell you they're absolutely fake," he said. "But damn expensive fakes, and aren't they gorgeous? They're just in case no one recognizes this as a jewelry case—"

"I didn't," admitted Mrs. Pollifax.

"—and they say to themselves, 'let's see if this is a geiger counter,' and they open it to find—presto, jewelry." He bent over the box. "See this tiny gold button on the hinge? Give it a good push and you'll have released the lock and can pull out the tray." He removed it and displayed a machine inside, a dial and two knobs set into a smooth metallic surface. He turned one of the knobs and they listened to a faint humming sound. "That's normal," he said. "Proves it's working and all that, and you're ready to pan for gold. The needle on the dial zooms, of course, when it sniffs out anything interesting. Check it out while I find your tickets, will you?"

Mrs. Pollifax closed, opened and closed the interior of the case. "It works," she said.

"Good—now I'll take it away from you."

"Take it away!"

"It'll be delivered to you on the plane when they hand

out the duty-free cigarettes and perfume that people have ordered. There's a rigorous search of every passenger boarding the plane and we'd rather not risk the wrong chap hauling you away for explanations."

"I see."

"I'm glad you do. And here are your tickets." He tapped a list with one finger as he studied it. "Tickets, jewel case, flashlight, batteries—"

"And violets," she reminded him. "Very handsome of you, too. I adore violets."

He glanced in amusement at her hat, which looked like a bathing cap overgrown with violets and pansies. "So I see. Is that thing called a cloche?"

"Bishop, you surprise me!"

"It's mutual. Oh yes—one more item here," he said. "The waiter Marcel." He brought a small photograph from his wallet and showed her a dark-haired, high cheekboned, gloomy face. "About five feet five. Broad-shouldered. There'll be a number of waiters and you'll want to know which one is Marcel. But avoid him, let him be the one to find you."

"Right," said Mrs. Pollifax efficiently, took a last glance and nodded.

"And that's about it," he concluded sadly. "So I daresay you'd better leave before too long a line forms at the check-in counter." He unlocked the door and opened it and then he closed the door again and said sternly, "You *will* take care? Not go around making citizens' arrests and that sort of thing? Just try to find the you-know-what and be well-behaved?"

"I shall feel I've behaved very well if I find the you-know-what," she told him.

He sighed. "Yes but I want to point out very strongly to you that any international crook who takes on this sort of game is tough and mercenary. Not your common ordinary garden type. Strictly jungle."

Mrs. Pollifax put down her suitcase and looked at him. "What's wrong, Bishop?"

"It's that obvious?" He scowled. "Hang it all, Carstairs didn't want you shaken up but I frankly think you ought to know."

"Know what?"

"The autopsy report on Fraser came in this noon, just before I left. The chap was dead before he fell down the mountainside."

"Before he fell," she repeated automatically.

"Yes. The actual blow that killed him couldn't possibly have come from any of the rocks he—uh—his body hit on the way down."

"I see," she said quietly. "You mean he was very definitely murdered."

"Yes."

She nodded. "Thank you for mentioning it, Bishop, I'll keep it in mind. You'll let me go now?"

"Reluctantly," he said, opening the door. "Very, very reluctantly."

Three

The code, when Mrs. Pollifax opened
it in the plane's lavatory, struck her as being really very funny. It read like Dick-and-Jane.

All is quiet—I AM GETTING RESTED.

I am worried—I HAVE A COUGH.

I feel I may be in danger—I BELIEVE I AM RUNNING A TEMPERATURE.

Below these simple sentences had been appended the following code names:

Marcel—COUSIN MATTHEW
Plutonium—UNCLE BILL
Police—PETER
Carstairs—ADELAIDE

After several trips to the lavatory she burned the code in an ashtray and returned to watch a Western film on the ingeniously placed moving picture screen. She had never before crossed the Atlantic and watched a film at the same time, and she was not sure that she approved of it. She enjoyed it but that, she felt, was not quite the same as approving of it. She wondered, for instance, how Columbus or Magellan would react if they could see them all sitting in comfortable chairs watching a movie in the sky as they crossed the ocean insulated from wind, tides, storm and distance, and without any decent sense of awe. One ought, she felt, to suffer just a little. Not much but a little.

As to Bishop's parting words she preferred not to think about them for the moment. He and Carstairs had each of them been right: it was kinder for her to know the worst, yet the news did have its jarring effect. Obviously Fraser's death meant there was something worth murdering for at Montbrison.

Long before the film ended the sky beyond her window had turned silver and she watched horizon-long bands of orange and pink dissolve into sunshine. It was only midnight in New York but they had crossed a time zone to meet Europe's dawn. Mrs. Pollifax made a last trip to the lavatory and then sat quietly attempting to enter her new role.

"I'm a mother-in-law recovering from the flu," she repeated to herself, and tried out an appropriate small cough . . . but a cough, codewise, meant that she was worried and was not to be confused with a flu cough. Her son-in-law was named Carstairs and he lived in Baltimore. There would be a limousine waiting for her, a delightful thought, and she would be whisked off to the Clinic—about an eighty-minute drive, Carstairs had said—and there she must look suitably tired.

Mrs. Pollifax coughed again, very delicately, and practised looking tired.

The driver of the limousine spoke almost no English. He drove silently and skillfully, and Mrs. Pollifax's attempts to compliment him on the weather lapsed. She stared out of the window at the countryside instead, at gentler mountains than she remembered seeing in the north, at red-tiled roofs and brief glimpses of a pale and shining Lake Geneva. They passed terraces of vineyards, villages just waking up—it was, after all, barely eight o'clock in the morning—and after an hour of driving they began to climb.

Mrs. Pollifax leaned forward eagerly. They were negotiating breathtakingly abrupt turns on a road that zigzagged high above the town and the lake; looking down she could see only the roofs of chalets, cottages and villas, and the tops of trees. Slowing somewhat they entered a village laid out at a 70-degree angle on the slopes of the mountain. Shops edged the slanting street, among them a cafe with umbrellas blossoming over rows of bright tables. The car turned down a narrow paved road, they passed a stone church clinging to the mountainside, a chalet, a few gardens and then entered a green-shaded wood with a ravine far below them on the right. Ahead Mrs. Pollifax saw a discreet sign: PRIVATE, it read. HOTEL-CLINIC MONTBRISON.

The driver cleared his throat and pointed. Mrs. Pollifax saw the rear of a large, rambling building almost suffocated by trees and shrubbery. They entered between two laurel bushes, drove down a steep narrow drive past a greenhouse, and arrived at the main door of the Clinic.

The sun had not yet reached the back of the building and the shadows were deep. At the entrance a stocky young man in a green apron was sweeping the steps with a broom while a small boy of ten or eleven sat on the top stair and watched him. Both looked up curiously at the limousine.

Mrs. Pollifax stepped out of the car. While the driver opened up the trunk to remove her suitcase she stood on the asphalt and glanced through the open door into the reception hall—it looked singularly gloomy with its dark paneling and rugs—and then the boy jumped up and called out shrilly, *"Bon jour, madame!"* This was followed by a torrent of words in French.

Mrs. Pollifax smiled and shook her head. "I'm sorry, I speak only English."

"But madame, I speak English, too," he told her, jumping up and down. "Why have you come? Are you to be a patient here? Are you English? Have you arrived by air? Why are you in that limousine? Will you stay long? Have you brought a nurse?"

A man in a black uniform appeared on the step, said something quieting to the boy in French and smiled at Mrs. Pollifax. "I am the head concierge, madame. Welcome to the Clinic. You are Madame Pollifax?"

She nodded.

"This way." He gave brisk orders to the man in the green apron, who dropped his broom and picked up Mrs. Pollifax's suitcase. "Please, you will come in and register, the secretary has not yet arrived in the office. It is very early, you see. Emil will show you to your room. You will wish breakfast, of course, it will be sent up to you at once."

He ushered her inside to the reception desk and held out paper and pen. Behind the desk she saw a switchboard, a wall of pigeonholes for mail and beyond that a pair of glass doors through which could be seen an empty office. She signed the register and handed over her passport.

"Yes, this I shall keep, it will be returned to you within

the hour," he said. He appeared refreshingly business-like, a little harassed and eminently likable. "May you enjoy your visit here, madame."

As she moved slowly upward in the elevator she looked down and saw the boy standing just inside the door staring after her. His brief excitement had collapsed; his eyes were huge and filled with a haunting sadness. She was glad when the ascent cut her off from his view.

Air and light was her first impression. As soon as Emil left, Mrs. Pollifax put down her jewelry case and crossed the room to open the door to her balcony. "Oh, *lovely,*" she whispered, moving to the railing. At this level she looked across the tops of high trees stirring in a light breeze. Beyond, and almost straight down, a toy steamer on the lake was disappearing between the treetops; it left behind it a V of tiny crepe paper wrinkles. Lake Geneva occupied the view almost to the horizon, like a pale blue, upside-down sky touched with glitter. A wash of insistent gray along the shores hinted at mountains still obscured by haze. Quiet morning sounds rose to her balcony: a tide-like rise and fall of traffic far away, birds calling, a muffled toot from the steamer, a church bell, all muted by distance and height.

She looked down in search of the garden, and had to stand on tiptoe to see over the wide jut of gallery that ran from her balcony to the next and continued along the floor to the end of the building. The broad ledge cut off much of the view below but she could see thick, well-kept grass, a circle of bright flowers, a graveled path overhung with pink roses, and a gazebo. The hush was incredible.

She turned and looked for her road and found it off to her left, just where Carstairs had said it would be, a narrow scar on the next hillside, unpaved and climbing at a precipitous angle. A flock of swallows interrupted her gaze. They dove in among the trees, almost encircling one tall Lombardy poplar, but they were the only sign of motion at Montbrison. Nothing seemed to move here, not even time.

I could be happy here, she thought, and found that she had to wrench her attention back to the reasons behind her arrival. Remembering, her glance fell to the ledge beyond the railing and she found herself studying it with interest. It was nearly four feet wide and neatly graveled. "Like a path three floors above the garden," she mused, and wondered if the other guests on her floor realized how accessible their rooms were. She thought it presented delightful possibilities for retreat or reconnaissance.

A knock on the door of her room distracted her. Reluctantly she left the balcony and walked inside, calling, "Come in."

A waiter in a white jacket entered, tray in hand. With a flourish he placed it on the tray table in the corner and wheeled the table to the center of the room. "Madame wishes it here, or on the balcony?"

"I think I'd fall asleep if I breakfasted on the balcony," she told him, and they exchanged a long and interested glance. He was a short and stocky young man, quite swarthy, with bright blue eyes and black hair parted in the center like a Victorian bartender. In Bishop's photograph he'd looked gloomy. He still looked gloomy but it was the sourness of a comedian who could fire off a string of ribald witticisms without a muscle quivering in his face. Marcel was something of a clown, she thought.

"I'll sit here," she said, and promptly sat down.

He wheeled the table beside her. "Madame has been sent the European *petit déjeuner*—very small," he explained with a rueful shrug. "If Madame wishes more she may dial the room service and a waiter will bring whatever she desires. I may pour your coffee, madame?" Before she could protest he leaned over and said in a low voice, "There is one particular counterfeit among the guests, madame, name of Robin Burke-Jones, usually in the garden afternoons, following three o'clock. We are most curious: none of his credentials check out, all data he gave upon registering is false."

"Thank you," said Mrs. Pollifax, smiling at him and nodding. "I think I have everything I need now."

"*Mon Dieu,* one hopes!" he said, returning to his humorous role. "If not—" He shrugged. "If not, the menu for service is on the desk. *Jambon ou lard, oeuf plat, oeuf poache sur toaste*—" His eyes were positively dancing at her. "My name is Marcel, madame. *Bon appetit!*" he said with a bow, and walked out.

My confederate, she thought, and was grateful to him for giving her something specific to do because a night without sleep had left her feeling jaded and just a little disoriented. She realized that she was also ravenous, and began to spread marmalade on her croissants. Over coffee she gazed around the room, which was cool, pale, and high-ceilinged, all white with small touches of blue and a deep red Oriental rug on the floor. Tonight, she decided, she would begin her explorations with the Geiger counter, and as her glance fell upon the bed, heaped high with pillows, she conceded that a brief morning nap would not be decadent.

Moving to the bed she saw that Marcel had left the door ajar, and that it was slowly opening wider. "Who's there?" she called out, and when no one answered she walked to the door.

"*Bon jour, madame,*" said the small boy she had seen at the entrance. He looked even smaller standing there, and more forlorn, his arms slack at his side. He lifted huge dark eyes to her face. "Would you be my friend, madame?" He pronounced the word *m'domm.*

She stared down at him in astonishment. "Are you a patient here?" she asked. He was very brown, very thin and wiry and leggy, with jet-black hair. In the small-boned dark face his eyes looked enormous. She had thought him the gardener's son.

He shook his head. "Grandmama is a patient and I am here to be with her. Have you grandchildren, madame?"

"Yes, three," she told him.

From somewhere down the hall a voice called, "Hafez? Hafez!"

The boy turned with a sigh. "Here, Serafina," he called.

A sallow-faced woman in black joined him in the framework of the door, took his hand, bent over him and admonished him in a language new to Mrs. Pollifax.

Hafez pushed out his underlip. "But this is my friend— one *must* have friends!" he cried, and there were tears in his eyes.

The woman pulled him away without so much as a glance at Mrs. Pollifax, who took a few steps into the hall to peer after them. Down at the far end of the hall, near the solarium, a man in a wheelchair sat watching the boy and the woman approach. Seeing Mrs. Pollifax he pushed his way back into the room behind him. Hafez and the woman went into the room opposite, two doors closed at once and there was silence.

A curious child, thought Mrs. Pollifax, the sound of his voice lingering in her ear.

She walked to the bed, lay down and fell asleep.

Twice she was awakened by knocks on the door, the first by a young woman in white who said she was a nurse but would return, the second time by a woman in white who said she was a dietician and would return. The third knock brought the secretary of the Clinic, a pigeon-breasted woman profuse with apologies at not having welcomed Mrs. Pollifax earlier. Seeing that it was eleven o'clock Mrs. Pollifax abandoned the idea of further sleep and got up. Lunch, said the secretary, was from noon to one o'clock, and dinner from six to eight. Mrs. Pollifax would be examined by a doctor tomorrow morning.

"Doctor? I'm only tired," pointed out Mrs. Pollifax.

"Ah, but it is the prerequisite, a how you say, a must? Everyone is examined, it is the rule of the Clinic. I understand also that you have not been weighed by the nurse yet, nor given menu instruction to the dietician." She shook her head reproachfully. "But you were tired?"

"I was asleep."

"Ah, yes," she murmured vaguely, and went out.

It occurred to Mrs. Pollifax that at such a pace the quietness of the Clinic might be illusion. She had been here in her room three hours, and had already received a nurse, a small boy, a dietician, a waiter, and a secretary. Tomorrow there would also be a doctor. Quickly she changed from her traveling suit to a dress and went downstairs to discover where lunch would be served, and to do a little reconnoitering before anyone else interrupted her.

She found solariums everywhere, all of them empty at this season of anything but jungle-like rubber plants. There were two more of them on the Reception floor, as well as a pair of television rooms side by side. The dining rooms lay at the far end of the corridor—Mrs. Pollifax could see the waiters moving past glass-paneled doors. She paused at what looked to be the library and glanced in at more dark, heavy furniture and rich oak paneling.

One piece of dark furniture was occupied by a handsome, deeply tanned young man who appeared to be examining the crease of his trouser. He glanced up and saw her, lifted an eyebrow and said, *"Bon jour, madame,* but that's the limit of my French."

"It's just about the limit of mine, too," she admitted, and decided this was an opportunity to meet her first adult guest. She sank into another large, overstuffed chair and wondered if she would ever be able to get out of it. "You're waiting for lunch, too?"

"I am waiting," he said gloomily, "for something to happen in this place. After eight days here I would consider the dropping of a spoon almost intolerable excitement."

Mrs. Pollifax looked at him with amusement. He just missed being impossibly handsome by a nose that had been broken and still looked a little stepped upon; she liked him the better for it because it gave humor to a face that was otherwise all tanned skin, sleepy green eyes, white teeth, and blond hair. "You do look as if you're accustomed to a faster pace," she admitted frankly.

"You're staring at my purple slacks and red shirt," he said accusingly. "I thought—I actually believed—Montbrison might have a touch of the Casino about it. After all, it's patronized by many of the same people, except when they come here it's to repair their livers. How was I to know that repairing the liver is almost a religion?"

"I had no idea," said Mrs. Pollifax, fascinated by the thought. "Is it?"

"My dear lady," he sighed, "I can only tell you that when I saw the Count Ferrari at Monaco in April he had a blonde in one hand and a pile of chips in the other. The count," he added, "is seventy-five if he's a day. Here at Montbrison he is suddenly mortal and positively devout about it. He carries pills. A whole *bag* full of pills. He dines across the room from me, and I swear to you he comes in every evening with a plastic bag of pills. You can see them: red, green, blue, pink."

Mrs. Pollifax laughed. "You're very observant but should you talk about your friend so loudly?"

"Oh, he's not a *friend,* he doesn't speak English," the young man said dismissingly. "We only say good evening to one another. I may not be a linguist—I confess to being stuffily British in that sense—but I can say good evening in approximately fifteen languages. Rather handy, that."

"Unless you meet them in the morning," she pointed out.

He grinned. "That, my dear lady, is a season of the day I avoid at any cost."

"If you're so bored—and if no one obliges you by dropping a spoon—and since you look so extremely healthy," she said, "Why do you stay?"

"Because my doctor sent me here." He hesitated and then added crisply, "I'm recovering from the Hong Kong flu, you see. And you?"

Mrs. Pollifax also found herself hesitating and then she said without expression, "Actually I'm recovering from the Hong Kong flu, too."

This ought to have produced instant commiseration, a few chuckles or a lively comparing of symptoms but it brought instead a flat, curiously awkward silence. I wonder why, she thought, and tried to find something to say. "I hear it was a particularly virulent strain last winter," she ventured.

"Uh—yes," he agreed, and suddenly aware of his clumsiness he began to speak when the doors of the dining room swung open. "Lunch!" he cried, springing to his feet. Very thoughtfully he helped her out of her chair. "You have to watch these chairs," he said sternly. "They're geared for sleep and that sort of thing. *Everything* is geared for sleep here, you can disappear forever in one of these damn things. Try the couch next time."

"I'll remember that," she told him gratefully. "By the way, I'm Mrs. Pollifax."

He bowed elegantly. "How do you do. And I'm—*Bon jour, mon General,*" he called out to an old man leaning heavily on a cane as he negotiated the hall to the dining room. "May I help you?" He was off like an Olympic runner to help the general, leaving Mrs. Pollifax with no name to attach to his acerbic personality.

In the dining room Mrs. Pollifax was guided to the table reserved for the occupant of room 113; the number was discreetly displayed on the shining damask cloth between the vase of wild flowers and the oil-and-vinegar tray. The table itself was placed in a corner of the first dining room, which gave her a strategic glimpse of those sharing her ell but no view at all of the other two rooms. The general was helped to a single table across from her in the center of the room and then her tanned young friend wandered off to his own table. Presently a subdued Hafez was brought in by the sallow woman in black and Mrs. Pollifax was surprised to see that they went to the long table for six by the window. It suggested a large party; he had mentioned a grandmother but the woman with him was not old enough, and gave every evidence of being a maid or companion. She wondered who the other people could be, and where they were.

She saw nothing of Marcel. Apart from Hafez and the general, only one other guest looked familiar and that was the man in the wheelchair whom she'd seen in the hall opposite Hafez's door. He wheeled himself to a solitary table nearby but facing the window so that she saw only his profile. It was not a particularly inspiring profile. His skin was dark but with a pallor that turned it to an unhealthy shade of gray. A thin black mustache decorated his lip, as if he reached for some longed-for sophistication that eluded him. His shoulders were massive and his business suit wrinkled. He looked out of place but indifferent to it; he ate quickly, with concentration, and wheeled himself out before Mrs. Pollifax reached her dessert.

Much more charming was the young girl who came in and sat opposite her across the room, and an older couple, the man with a London *Times* under his arm.

"I must learn something about all of them," she reminded herself. Marcel had mentioned the garden; she would spend the afternoon in the garden.

Four

The garden was bright with sun and flowers. With a professional eye Mrs. Pollifax inspected the beds of begonias along the paths and then headed for a chaise longue and sank into it, hoping that she wouldn't fall asleep. Just to be certain of this she climbed out of the chaise and attempted to elevate it to a sitting position.

"You're pushing all the wrong things," said a voice behind her, and a young woman in a bikini, body glistening with sun oil, put down her towel and books and leaned over the chair. It sprang back and up immediately.

Mrs. Pollifax smiled. "How efficient you are!"

"I am, yes," the girl said with a touch of rue in her voice. "Do you think that's an affliction or a gift?"

"A little bit of each, I should think," hazarded Mrs. Pollifax. "You're British?"

She shook her head. "Belgian."

"I saw you in the dining room, you sat opposite me," added Mrs. Pollifax by way of introduction. "I'm Mrs. Pollifax."

"How do you do," the girl said, and extended a thin brown hand. "I'm Court van Roelen." Her face was all cheekbones and angles, with a pair of eyes that blazed like blue jewels in her tanned face. It was a breathtaking combination.

Over the girl's head—she was surprisingly small—Mrs. Pollifax saw that her nameless male friend of the library was standing in the center of the lawn staring open-

35

mouthed at the girl. He too seemed to find her breathtaking. He was now wearing yellow slacks, an orange shirt, and a polka-dotted cravat but the effect was entirely spoiled by his gaping. Closing his mouth he strolled toward Mrs. Pollifax. "I think a spoon just dropped," he said.

"I could hear the reverberations," she told him.

He grinned. "Don't let me interrupt anybody's sun bath, I'll just pull this young lady's chair closer and we can turn this into a cozy threesome." Beaming at Mrs. Pollifax he added, "Numerologically, you know, three is a number of great strength." Leaving no time for a reply he drew up a third chair, into which he settled complacently. "You were about to introduce us?" he asked Mrs. Pollifax with a lift of his brow.

"I will if you'll tell me your name."

He looked startled. "Oh, sorry about that. Burke-Jones is the name. Robin Burke-Jones."

Mrs. Pollifax gave him a quick glance; she had made a better choice than she'd realized in her first adult encounter. Performing introductions she settled back to see what would happen next.

"I haven't seen you before," Burke-Jones told the girl. "You've just arrived?"

"I've been here for ten days," she said coolly, "but I've been on the mountain every day hiking."

"Hiking," he echoed. "What do you mean hiking? There's nothing restful about hiking."

"I don't come here to rest," she said. "It's my vacation, and I prefer to avoid resorts, they're always so full of—" For just a second her glance rested on his exquisitely arranged cravat. "So full of playboys."

"Well, well," he said, beaming at her, "we must discuss this further."

"I don't see why," she retorted and turned over on her stomach to tan her back.

"Speaking of playboys," added Mrs. Pollifax wickedly, "what do you do, Mr. Burke-Jones?"

"Spend my time envying playboys," he said virtuously. "Actually, since you ask, I'm in the import business. Curios and knickknacks." He lifted an arm to wave at the general, whom a nurse was helping into a chair not far away. "A shop in Brighton, another in Dover, branches here and there," he added vaguely. "And you, Miss van Roelen? You are not, I take it, a playgirl?"

Her voice was muffled against the towel on which her cheek rested. "Administrative assistant, UNESCO."

"Oh, very worthy," he murmured, and lifted a brow at Mrs. Pollifax. "Wouldn't you say so, too?"

He was really impossible, she thought, and also rather nice but he was going to have a problem with Miss van Roelen. "Extremely so," she told him, and wondered what he really did. She did not for a moment believe in his import business, and considering Marcel's warning she saw no reason why she should.

The glass doors to the garden had opened and Hafez was arriving, dressed in a fresh pair of shorts and white shirt and carrying a shiny black box. The servant appeared like a shadow behind him and took a chair under a tree. Hafez placed his box on the glass and began fiddling with knobs and a small microphone. From this distance it looked like a tape recorder.

Abruptly Court sat up and called out to a woman strolling down the graveled path. "Oh, Lady Palisbury—"

This woman too had shared Mrs. Pollifax's dining room but she had been with her husband then. Mrs. Pollifax watched her pause and her face brighten at sight of Court. "Hello, there," she called, cutting across the lawn toward them. "I've been walking in the ravine." Under a huge sun hat a pair of deep-set wise eyes smiled at them.

"I just wanted to ask, did you find your missing diamond?"

Lady Palisbury shook her head. "No, my dear, but it will turn up, I'm sure."

"I almost inquired at lunch, but your husband—"

"Quite thoughtful of you, dear. No, I don't want to worry him, his blood pressure would skyrocket. John is a very impulsive man," she added, her mouth curving humorously.

"Lady Palisbury, this is Mrs. Pollifax and Mr. Burke-Jones."

She nodded pleasantly. "But I'm not going to join you, no matter how comfortable you look. I'm on my way in to wake up my husband. He has a massage at four."

"Boom, boom, boom," shouted Hafez suddenly, streaking across the garden toward the glass doors. "Monsieur?" he shouted to a waiter. *"Un Coca-Cola!"*

Lady Palisbury strolled away. As she passed Hafez he held up the tiny microphone, the tape recorder cradled under his arm, and spoke to her in French. Lady Palisbury smiled, graciously took his microphone and spoke into it before she disappeared inside.

"Does his grandmother ever keep him company?" asked Mrs. Pollifax, watching Hafez fly off in another direction.

"Whose grandmother?"

"The boy's."

"Didn't know he had one," said Burke-Jones.

"It must be terribly dull for him here," Court said, sitting up and hugging her knees. "What would he be, ten, eleven?"

"He's so small it's difficult to guess. He said he was here with his grandmother, who's a patient."

"I suspect he's rather brilliant," said Court thoughtfully. "I don't know when he sleeps—he's all nerves, isn't he?— because he's one guest I met consistently at six o'clock in the morning, when I was leaving for my walks. He told me yesterday about pulsars. Stars, you know—or planets, I forget which."

"Mmm," said Mrs. Pollifax, watching the boy approach the general under the tree.

The general, too, was being kind; he spoke into the microphone and Hafez laughed. There was a shrill note to his laughter and Mrs. Pollifax studied the boy as he implored the general to say more.

Court laughed. "He has persuaded the general to say, *'Ici la police—sortez, les mains en l'air!'* which means 'Come out with your hands up, this is the police speaking.' The general," she added, "was once the head of the Sûreté."

Robin looked startled. "I thought he was just a regular military general."

"He was a general during World War Two, under de Gaulle. Then he became head of the Sûreté."

"So he's a French police chief," murmured Mrs. Pollifax, watching Robin's face speculatively.

He said crossly, "How do you happen to know so much about everybody, Miss van Roelen, when you don't know anything about me?"

Court actually smiled at him. "I came here last summer and liked it, you see, and the general was a patient here then, too. He's very old and very alone and he hasn't much longer to live."

But it was now their turn with Hafez, who was suddenly in front of them thrusting his microphone at each of them in turn and shrilly demanding that they say something.

"I'll volunteer, Hafez," said Mrs. Pollifax, and he came eagerly to her side. She lifted the microphone, thought a moment and then recited an old nursery rhyme.

"Edward Lear!" exclaimed Court, delighted. "Here, Hafez, take me next." And into the microphone, with a smile at Mrs. Pollifax she recited, " 'There was an Old Man with a beard, who said It is just as I feared! Two Owls, and a Hen, Four Larks and a Wren, Have all built their nests in my Beard.' "

"I prefer the general's announcements to your frivolous

limericks," said Robin, and grasping the microphone he called, "Come out with your hands high—the jig is up!"

But Mrs. Pollifax's glance had returned to Hafez because there remained something puzzling about him that she could not explain to herself. His eyes were far too bright, of course, his gestures quick and nervous but there was more to it than this; she realized his gestures were curiously without meaning. *He doesn't really know what he's doing*, she thought, watching him; *he doesn't care, either, he acts for the sake of being in motion*. Her gaze fell to his hands as he returned the mike to the tape recorder and she saw that they were trembling. She realized that the boy was living under an intolerable weight of tension.

"Tiresome brat," said Robin when the boy had dashed off to intercept others in the garden.

"Overactive thyroid?" suggested Court, lying down again.

"No," said Mrs. Pollifax slowly, "No, it's more than that. Much more, I think." She was remembering her own children, and a time when Roger was six and booked for a tonsillectomy, and a playmate had told him the doctor would smother him with a pillow in the operating room. Roger had lived with that terror for two days before he had entrusted it to her but even now she did not care to remember those two days.

Both heads turned to her expectantly. "I think he's frightened," she said, and was startled to hear herself say it.

"Frightened?" echoed Court doubtfully. "What could possibly frighten a child here?"

"Frankly, it's he who frightens me," said Robin with a grin.

Mrs. Pollifax only shook her head and said nothing, but now that she had identified the emotion that possessed the boy she felt that she might even have underestimated it. He was not just frightened, she decided, watching him, he was desperately, nightmarishly afraid.

*   *   *

Dinner that evening was something called *sauté de veau marengo,* which turned out to be veal, and Mrs. Pollifax began to think of buying a French dictionary. In her youth she had studied Latin and a smattering of Greek, neither of which seemed to be of much help to her in contemporary life. From each she had learned something of the beauty and history of language but she had forgotten every scrap of her Latin with the exception of the phrase *Fortes fortuna iuvat,* or Fortune favors the bold. It was a phrase that contained a certain amount of comfort for her now, as she considered at what nocturnal hour she should begin her prowlings.

"You're new," said Lady Palisbury as the two of them sat in the library, Mrs. Pollifax over her demitasse, Lady Palisbury knitting as she waited for her husband to join her for dinner.

"This morning, yes. Ever so early. Straight from the plane."

"You come so far," murmured Lady Palisbury with a curious glance at her over her knitting.

"I have an internationally minded son-in-law," Mrs. Pollifax told her with a smile.

Lady Palisbury brightened. "Oh, how nice. We have four, and all darlings. They're so soothing after a household of daughters, all of whom are darlings, too, but given to shrieks and squeals and quarrels and so forth." She had an amiable way of talking, with frequent glances into the hall. "I fervently hope Women's Lib will give my daughters what I couldn't. When one has never been afraid of frogs and mice and spiders—and begets four daughters terrified of them—one begins to question chromosomes." She glanced up anxiously. "I do wish John would come before we get involved with the yodelers."

"Yodelers?" said Mrs. Pollifax, startled.

"You didn't see the sign in the hall? It's Friday night, you see, and the clinic arranges"—her mouth curved— "little weekend entertainments for us. Tomorrow there will probably be a film in the dining room, Sunday, of course, is visitors' day and tonight there are yodelers from the village."

"How very neighborly," commented Mrs. Pollifax. She had been watching the hall and her attention sharpened as Hafez and his companion left the dining room.

"You're curious about the boy," said Lady Palisbury, following her glance.

"He looks tonight as if he'd been crying," explained Mrs. Pollifax. "Do you know anything about him?"

Lady Palisbury turned over the sweater she was knitting and counted stitches before she replied. "I know they're Zabyans," she said, "but don't ask me which country Zabya is, I get those Arabian countries terribly mixed up. Oil, I think—yes, it's one of the oil countries, and there's a king. He was in the news recently, something about a birthday party and giving away all the royal land to his people."

Mrs. Pollifax nodded. "I remember that. A nice little man. At least he seemed to be *trying*."

"Very short in stature," nodded Lady Palisbury, "but long in courage. Oh dear, the yodelers are here."

The yodelers had indeed arrived, a group of plump, embarrassed, beaming villagers, the women in brightly embroidered dirndls and the men in high socks, shorts, and feathered hats. Lady Palisbury's husband stood in their midst looking equally as embarrassed and quite helpless. He separated himself from the yodelers and presented himself to his wife. "My dear, who *are* they?" he whispered.

"There you are, darling," said Lady Palisbury, putting away her knitting. "This is Mrs. Pollifax, John."

"Splendid," he said absently. "But Jane—"

"Yodelers, dear," she whispered, and as they moved into the dining room the group of performers followed; seconds later the sounds of strident yodels filled the air.

"Good God, have we been invaded?" asked Burke-Jones, strolling in from the solarium.

"Only by folk culture," she told him. "I think it's rather endearing."

He shuddered. "Not to me. Look, I'm driving down to the village for cigarettes—I have my car with me here—and I'll be gone only ten or fifteen minutes. Would you care to come?" He added casually, "I thought I'd ask Court, too."

Mrs. Pollifax smiled faintly. "It's half-past eight and I'm getting sleepy after losing a night's sleep on the plane. I think she's in the dining room."

"Who?"

"Court, of course."

Barely smothering a yawn she bid him good night and went upstairs.

She had left the doors to her room closed; there were two of them, a thick one padded with quilted fabric for soundproofing and an inner conventional one that could be locked. Both stood ajar now, and seeing this Mrs. Pollifax quickened her step. It might be only a chambermaid turning down the bed, or it could be Marcel.

It was neither. It was the boy Hafez, sitting in front of the glass-topped desk and hunched over something in his lap.

"Hafez," she said indignantly, "you simply mustn't walk in and out of rooms when people aren't in them."

His hands quickly returned something to the desk; whatever it was she heard it click against the glass top before he jumped to his feet to face her. "But, madame," he said, "I have been waiting for you. You did not say if you decided to be my friend."

"I would be delighted to be your friend," she told him, "but friends always knock before they come into a room."

"But, madame, I did knock," he protested. "It's just that I received no answer."

"Because I wasn't here."

"But where else could I have waited?" he asked, a desperate note creeping into his voice. "Serafina would have been very angry, she would have taken me off to bed if she saw me in the hall."

"Do you like Serafina?"

The child shrugged; whatever troubled him it was not Serafina. "Must you tell her I came inside?"

"No, but only because we're going to be friends, except you simply mustn't come in uninvited or we can't be friends."

He considered this and nodded. "Thank you," he said, and astonished her by walking out and closing both doors behind him.

Mrs. Pollifax stood looking after him, completely baffled, and then she sat down at the desk where Hafez had been sitting. Its contents were meager: a hairbrush, a jar of cold cream, a small bottle of aspirin, an address book, a lipstick, and the magazines she had read on the plane but not yet tossed into the wastebasket. She shared Court's impression of Hafez's intelligence and she did not feel that his visit had been entirely impulsive. She wanted to know which of these objects had caught his attention and which had clicked against the glass as he put it back.

She picked up the lipstick and examined it but it appeared untouched. She leaned closer to the aspirin and then she picked it up and held it to the light. She had bought it just before leaving, a small supply of twenty-five tablets in case of emergency. It looked only half-filled now. She removed the plug of cotton and poured the tablets into the palm of her hand. There were only twelve left. As she returned the bottle to the desk it clicked against the glass with a matching familiarity. Of course—glass against glass.

She shook her head. In a clinic where any nurse could supply aspirin, why did Hafez feel compelled to steal thirteen tablets, she wondered. Did he just—take things, like a kleptomaniac? She sat and frowned at the bottle, exasperated by her bewilderment; she realized that she would have to make a point of meeting Hafez's grandmother soon.

And then she found herself wondering what sort of grandmother would bring a small boy to the Clinic—a clinic of all places—when he ought to be at home playing with children of his own age. The old could be very selfish, she conceded, but it was possible the woman had no idea the child was disturbed.

I wonder, she thought idly, and glanced at her watch. It lacked a few minutes to nine and she did not have to signal with her flashlight until ten. Downstairs the yodelers were still at work, their lusty high notes penetrating the building, so obviously the social hour remained in force. I'll just pay a neighborly call, she thought. I'll make no judgments, I'll just *see*.

Resolutely she left her room and walked down the hall to knock on the door that Hafez had entered that morning. Hafez opened the door and a look of utter astonishment passed over his face. "Madame?" he faltered, and astonishment was followed by alarm. "Madame?" he repeated.

"Since we're friends I thought I'd pay a brief call on your grandmother," she told him cheerfully, and walked past him. "I trust she's well enough to—but where?" she asked, seeing that she was entering an obviously unoccupied room. Her glance swerved to an open door on the left, and then to an open door on her right.

Hafez said, "But, madame—" His glance leaped anxiously to the left, and Mrs. Pollifax followed it.

Somewhere a man's voice called out sharply in another language, and Hafez replied. There was the sound of glass falling to the floor, and an oath, followed by movement. Mrs. Pollifax reached the threshold of the adjoining bedroom and stopped. She had time to meet the shocked glance of Serafina, and time to glimpse the occupant of the bed in the darkened corner, and then she was seized from

behind. A man grabbed her left elbow, another her right
elbow, and lifting her off the floor she was carried, still
erect, to the door. It happened so quickly that her breath
was literally taken away from her, and with it her voice.

"Ukhrujee," said the one burly attendant. *"Maksala-
mah!"*

She was shoved roughly outside. Across the hall the
man in the wheelchair sat and watched with narrowed
eyes. She noticed that his hands gripped the arms of his
chair so tightly that the knuckles were white. He muttered
something, retreated and closed the door.

Mrs. Pollifax groped her way to one of the chairs lining
the corridor and sank into it, shaken by the experience.
After a few minutes she made her way down the hall to
her room and closed the door behind her. She did not
know whether to feel shocked, angry, or penitent. At the
moment she felt a little of each and wondered which
would triumph. "This isn't New Brunswick, New Jersey,"
she reminded herself, and then fiercely. "All right what
could you expect, Emily? Of course they were outraged.
Obviously the woman isn't well and these servants or rela-
tives, or whoever they are, have come to see that she has
the best of care and of course they're shocked to find a
stranger bursting into the room without invitation."

Of course.

So much for penitence.

The woman had lain in bed, very pale and fragile in her
sleep: long braided gray hair, a slightly curved nose, a
good jaw, eyes closed. Serafina had been sitting near her
but half out of her chair at sight of Mrs. Pollifax. The two
attendants apparently stayed in the farther room, and
Hafez had been given the middle one. The grandmother,
in the third room, had not even known of Mrs. Pollifax's
arrival—hadn't even stirred—but the man in the wheelchair across the hall had known. It had never occurred to
her that he might be a member of the party.

And Hafez . . . he had been astonished to see her, and

then alarmed, but he had made no move to stop her and as she had been carried out of the room she had glimpsed his face and he had looked pleased. Pleased by what, her coming to pay a call, or by her ejection?

She had expected—admit it—a querulous old woman, spoiled, vain, and doting on a grandson she needed but could neither entertain nor supervise. Instead she had found a still white face lying on a white pillow, and two angry attendants. She must ask Marcel; perhaps he could explain this.

She glanced at her watch and walked out to her balcony into a velvety stillness. Far below the lighted garden the lake was black and silent except for a lone steamer making its way to port; it trailed behind it ribbons of gold. It was peaceful here, it steadied her. The curving shores on either side twinkled with the lights of casinos and villas. On her left the adjacent hillside was no more than a brooding silhouette. She held her wrist to the light and checked the time.

At precisely ten o'clock she switched on her flashlight, counted to three, turned it off, then on, then off, and was startled and pleased to see that a pair of headlights sprang into life on the hillside. They illuminated the road like twin beams from a lighthouse so that she could see bushes, the trunk of a tree, the texture of the rough dirt road, and above all the angle at which the road dropped, and which the car now proceeded to follow down, dipping lower and lower until it vanished behind a stand of trees.

Whoever you are, she thought, it *is* nice to know you're there.

In the garden below, one of the gardeners was turning off the spotlights hidden among the flower beds. One by one they died, and darkness joined with the stillness. The Clinic was being put to bed.

It was time for her to get to work, she realized, and time to forget her impulsive and abortive call on Hafez.

Five

In Langley, Virginia, it was half-

past four in the afternoon and Carstairs was only finishing his morning's work. He had begun the day with a tightly organized schedule but in midmorning the State Department had urgently requested a report on one of the smaller oil countries in the Middle East. It seemed the King of Zabya was celebrating his fortieth birthday on Tuesday, and a good many heads of state were attending the day-long festivities. Was the country stable enough for America to send the Vice-President, or should an expendable diplomat be dispatched in his place? Carstairs's comments on this during the afternoon had become increasingly un-printable but the report had been completed and delivered: the Vice-President could be sent but he would have to expect boiled sheeps' eyes on the menu.

Bishop wandered into the office smothering a yawn. "Schoenbeck's outside," he said.

"I thought you'd left."

"I'm leaving now. Schoenbeck's flying back to Geneva in two hours, he wants to wrap things up before he goes."

"Right. I don't suppose there's coffee?"

Bishop brightened. "As a matter of fact it's the only thing that's kept me intelligent, charming, and alive these past hours. Shall I bring in Schoenbeck?"

"*And* the coffee," added Carstairs.

Schoenbeck was Interpol, a rather pedantic little man with a lined face. He came in now, murmuring a thousand apologies for the intrusion and when courtesies had been dispensed with Carstairs offered him coffee and sat down.

"Gervard's going to be in charge at the Lake Geneva end," began Schoenbeck. "He's the man to contact if anything comes up. I won't be seeing you again, I'll be in Geneva."

"Anything changed?"

"My friend, everything changes," said Schoenbeck. "It is the law of life. I have just learned that it is useless for me to go to England for any new interrogations, the Dunlap man committed suicide this morning."

Carstairs swore gently. "How the hell could he commit suicide in a prison cell, wasn't he being watched?"

Schoenbeck shrugged. "The cessation of life, my friend, does not take long. He hung himself swiftly with a bedsheet. A frightened man, obviously. Suddenly more frightened of life than of death."

They were both silent, contemplating this. "No," said Carstairs, shaking his head, "more frightened of *them* than of us. Two ordinary working men, one in England, one in America, and nothing in common except they happened to work in a nuclear reactor plant—and succumbed to stealing two buttons each of plutonium."

"There is another thing they had in common, my friend," said the man from Interpol. "Both wanted very much to live—at least greed always disposes me to think thus—and both have killed themselves before we could discover any other links to this chain."

Carstairs nodded gloomily. "And their widows are richer. Anything yet on the money?"

Schoenbeck shook his head. "Not a thing, except that— *voilà!*—each has a bank account that is magically bulging. It must have been dealt over in cash. A dead end."

Carstairs sighed. "Well organized."

"Indeed yes." Schoenbeck, looking stern, put down his coffee cup. "It pains me, my friend, that we know so little, that all of it is based on scraps. We know that in each case the plutonium was tossed over the wall during working hours by a workman. We learn that in England a green sedan was seen by a farmer parked beside that wall about the right time, and the same green sedan was seen twenty minutes after the theft parked in front of the village post office—"

"But Stokely-on-the-Merden *is* a small village," pointed out Carstairs.

"Oh yes, small enough so that the postal clerk recalls a stranger mailing a crate to Switzerland that day to a clinic near St. Gingolph named Mont-something. But everything we have is based on the word of a farmer plowing his fields, two housewives gossiping in front of a post office and the vulnerable memory of a postal clerk."

Carstairs smiled forgivingly at his friend. "You're feeling discouraged, Monsieur Schoenbeck. How often do you have more solid leads? What do we ever work with but scraps and pieces? Yet the world lurches on."

"It is my concern over its continuing to lurch that troubles me," remarked Schoenbeck. "This is a dangerous time to have plutonium drifting about loose in the world, there is too much hate. Your agent is now joining ours at Montbrison?"

Carstairs glanced at his watch. "Yes, as a matter of fact she would have been there for some hours now."

Schoenbeck nodded. "Good. We have discovered, by the way, a clinic called Montrose some forty miles to the south, and we are putting an agent in there as well, whom Gervard will supervise. We will, of course, continue to follow every small possibility concerning the two men who stole the plutonium. The dead can no longer speak but their friends have not lost that power. What I want from you, my friend—"

Carstairs lifted his brows. "More?" he asked with comic despair.

"There is always more. I want from you an alert, a query, transmitted to all your agents around the world, barring none. It troubles me deeply that we hear no hints of this in the marketplaces of the world. In Beirut, Marseilles, and New York we hear not a whisper. This is most exceptional, a group this organized turning to this type of crime and no informants, no leaks, no tips."

"Queries everywhere?"

"Everywhere, if you please. The plutonium has to find a market eventually, does it not? And we *must* know who is buying it. Otherwise, my friend," he said flatly, "the balance of power will tip, slide, and perhaps send us all into oblivion."

"You still believe it's one of the international crime syndicates, forsaking drugs for plu—" The telephone interrupted Carstairs and he reached over to pick it up and bark his name into it. "What? Yes, he's here," he said, and handed the telephone to Schoenbeck. "You keep your office well-informed," he commented dryly.

Schoenbeck, smiling, took the phone. He listened, replied in rapid French, listened again and seemed to visibly sag in his chair. *"Oui,"* he added, and hung up. "Well, my friend, I must go," he said, standing up. An ironic smile played over his lined and weary face. "That was Geneva calling. There has been a third theft of plutonium."

"What?" thundered Carstairs.

"Yes, a third. In France this time. Two how-you-call-it metal buttons of plutonium, each weighing a kilogram." He leaned over and picked up a pencil. "A kilogram in pounds is 2.2046 for your edification, my friend. Six kilograms are now missing." He was figuring with the pencil and paper, and at last he held it out to Carstairs.

Carstairs reached for it and whistled. "Thirteen pounds and two ounces altogether," he said.

Schoenbeck nodded. "They now have their atom bomb," he said. "I leave you, my friend, but I think you will find me in France, not Geneva. In the meantime— *c'est la guerre*. Literally."

He went out, leaving Carstairs thoughtful and depressed.

Six

Earlier, during dinner, Mrs. Pollifax had mentally compiled a list of what to avoid: the elevator, of course, which purred almost silently but still sent out vibrations of movement and whispering cables; the night concierge or whoever manned the counter and telephones at night; and she supposed that someone—somewhere—must be available for patients who were restless. She would have to discover for herself where the pockets of activity lay at night.

She changed into pajamas and robe and checked the jewelry box, leaving the tray inside but removing the jewels and tucking them into her pocket. "Fortune favors the bold," she reminded herself as she looked out on the dimly lighted, deserted hall. For one overwhelming moment she longed to retreat and go to bed and then she remembered Fraser. She walked down the hall to the elevator and took the broad, carpeted stairs beside it to the Reception floor. The switchboard was unmanned and the concierge's counter empty. She stood a moment listening and heard a low murmur from the television room; the night porter had forsaken his post for a program. Quietly she followed the stairs down and around to the ground floor. This was the unknown, a rabbit warren of therapy and equipment rooms, offices, baths and pools and the kitchen. It was also, she felt, the most likely place in which to hide anything illicit, especially if it had been labeled MEDICAL SUPPLIES.

Down here the lights had not been dimmed and the brightly lighted hall alarmed her; before doing anything else she looked for a hiding place. An unmarked door concealed a utility room that was mercifully dark, and she slipped inside. Her flashlight moved across tubs, pails, brooms, mops, and a wall filled with fuse boxes and circuit breakers. From this vantage point she opened the door a few inches and waited, listening.

To her right, far down the hall, someone had begun to whistle monotonously through his teeth. The sound came from the kitchen but the frosted-glass doors remained closed; a pastry chef, she decided, baking for the next day. Turning on the Geiger counter she slipped back into the hall and tiptoed to the wide swinging doors at the far end labeled HYDROTHERAPIES.

HYDROTHERAPIES was a large room dark and almost gymnasium-size, and occupied by two round tile pools filled with water that gleamed under her flashlight. Whirlpool baths, she guessed as she moved slowly around the sides. A glance at the luminous dial of the counter showed the needle quiet. She opened a door in the wall and walked into an office; here she spent several minutes investigating the closets. A second office stood next to it, followed by a room marked UNTERWASSER MASSAGE. With some curiosity she entered the latter and found a large, rectangular green tub standing in the center of the room, raised on a platform. Pipes and formidable-looking tubes surrounded it, and over the faucets a series of dials added to the impression that she had stumbled into a medieval torture chamber. Here, too, water stood in the tub, very still and filled with moving light. It was strange how alive and sinister water could look at night, she thought, and with relief opened the door to the hall.

She had now completed the east wing of the ground floor, which was separated from the opposite wing by the lobby containing the staircase, elevator, and entrance doors to the garden. As she peered into the lobby from the

Unterwasser Massage door she drew back hastily, surprised at discovering that she was not the only prowler in the night. Barely six feet away from her someone was trying to get into the building from the garden. She could hear the click and rustle of tools at work; the intruder was picking the lock. Mrs. Pollifax turned off her scintillator counter and waited.

There was a last muffled click and the door swung open. Marcel slipped inside.

"Marcel!" she gasped in relief.

He jumped and crossed himself before he saw her standing in the shadows of the Unterwasser Massage room. "You scare the devil from me, madame!"

"Sorry—you frightened me, too. Whatever are you doing picking the lock?"

His face turned wry. "Waiters are not allowed keys, madame—and I am a waiter. It makes for much difficulty, especially when I am off duty." He moved away from the glass door to the garden and joined her in the darkness. "I have spent the last hour seated in the garden, in the darkness, watching. Have you been down here long? Have you seen or heard anyone?"

"Only the person in the kitchen working. Why?"

"I swear to you I saw someone on the roofs of the building a few minutes ago." He frowned. "It is very dark out there, with no moon, but still—" He shook his head. "I do not like it."

"And you want to look around," she said approvingly. "But first—really it's providential, meeting you, Marcel. I can borrow you for a minute?"

He grinned. "For eternity, madame! I may be of service?"

"Yes. You know Hafez?"

He sighed. *"Mon Dieu,* who does not?" He lifted his eyes heavenward.

"He seems very upset, even frightened. I tried to pay a call on his grandmother less than an hour ago, to speak to her about it." She shivered. "I was carried bodily out of the room by two men."

He whistled faintly. "That is surprising and not very hospitable. Let me think. The Zabyan party," he said thoughtfully. "They occupy rooms 150, 152, 154. Their meals are served to them in their rooms with the exception of the boy and the maid. I have myself delivered some of the meals, but only to room 154, where a man in white jacket accepts the trays." He closed his eyes. "Their names are—yes, I have it—Madame Parviz and grandson Hafez, Serafina Fahmy, Fouad Murad, and Munir Hassan." He opened his eyes. "Other than this, I know nothing. They were not investigated further because, you see, they were not guests here when Fraser was killed."

It was Mrs. Pollifax's turn to frown. "You're quite sure of that?"

"Quite, madame. They arrived that same day, shortly after, but they were not here at that time. I will, of course, make inquiries further."

"Oh please do," she told him. "And there's one other thing: When can I get into the kitchen?"

His glance fell to the jewelry case and he smiled. "Ah, yes I see. But tonight no. Saturday—tomorrow—yes, there will be no one here then." He glanced toward the stairs. "I must go," he said. "Give me five minutes to get past the night porter. Technically I have been off duty four hours, and should be in my room in the village."

He moved to the stairs, listened a moment, and then with a wave of his hand to her vanished.

She reflected that she had at least learned the name of Hafez's grandmother, and that Marcel was vigilantly on guard outside the Clinic. She turned on her scintillator counter and crossed the hall to the door marked LABORATORIES. Inside this door lay a long narrow hall with small rooms opening from it. Of particular interest was the large storage room at the end of the hall. Her flashlight roamed past crates of peaches, spices, chocolate, and coffee. Another row contained crates of sterile cotton and cardboard cartons from various drug laboratories of Europe, none of them causing any change on her counter. At the far corner she found an aluminum chute standing against the wall, and above it a window of an exact size to fit both the chute and the crates. She realized this was where supplies were unloaded. The window would be opened, the chute locked in place, the crates taken from a truck and sent sliding into the basement. She stood on a box and peered out of the window; her flashlight picked out cement and a lattice-work trellis. Tomorrow she would look for the window from the outside.

She had given Marcel his allotted five minutes. Denied the kitchen she began to have pleasant thoughts of bed, and returning to the lobby ascended the stairs to the Reception floor. This time, however, she was not so fortunate. The night concierge stood at his post by the switch-board leafing through a magazine. Shocked, he gasped, "Madame!" and rattled off a string of words in French, all of them alarmed.

She said firmly, "I've been looking for someone to take care of my emeralds." She removed the pendant from her pocket and placed it on the counter between them. "I saw a sign while I was brushing my teeth—in the bathroom, you understand—that said all valuables should be placed in your safe. How could I possibly sleep after reading that?"

He understood English; he nodded but he had trouble removing his eyes from the play of light across the emeralds. "But, madame," he countered, "I have no key. Only the head concierge can open the safe. I am sadly sorry. At seven he is on duty."

"Oh," she said. "Oh well." She put away the pendant with regret. *"Bon soir,* then."

"Yes, madame—and try to sleep a little? At seven he comes."

She nodded and continued up the stairs to her own

floor. As she opened the door to room 113 she glanced down the hall and saw Hafez standing silently outside his room watching her. He was too far away for her to see his face clearly; he simply stood there, still dressed in white shorts and shirt, and then he turned abruptly and disappeared.

It was 12:05. The Clinic, thought Mrs. Pollifax, seemed to have a hidden but vivid night life of its own.

Locking her door she climbed into bed, reflected that she had at least made a beginning, and on that note fell asleep, entering a dream where she wandered through a labyrinth of dark rooms, each of them colder by degrees until she reached a hall thick with white frost. In her sleep Mrs. Pollifax stirred restlessly, and shivered.

She opened her eyes to find that a cold wind had sprung up and was blowing through the door to the balcony, presenting her with the choice of getting up and closing the door or getting up to look for a blanket. Neither prospect appealed, she wanted only to sleep. As she lay and rebelliously considered these alternatives a curious thought occurred to her: she had not left the balcony door open, she had closed and locked it.

A moment later she realized that not only was the door open but that someone else was in her room with her.

Seven

Her awareness was a combination of sixth sense and of those nearly imperceptible but speaking sounds comprised of motion, faint rustlings, and haste. She remembered the lamp sitting only a few feet away from her on the night table and tried to slowly disengage her right hand from its tangle of sheets. If she could reach the lamp before her unknown guest heard the rustling of the covers—

Over by the desk a thin beam of light appeared down near the floor, a light scarcely broader than a hairline. Caution vanished. Mrs. Pollifax freed her hands, swept back the sheets, switched on the light and stared in astonishment. "You!" she cried.

Robin Burke-Jones slowly rose to his feet from the floor. "Damn it, yes," he said, looking shaken.

"And through my balcony door—"

"Sorry about that. I suppose you want my hands up and all that?"

"If you'll feel more comfortable that way," she told him, groping for her slippers and wondering exactly where and how he fitted into this. Marcel had warned her, of course, but still she admitted a deep sense of disappointment because she had liked this young man. "At the moment I'd prefer to know just what you're doing in my room at"—she glanced at the clock—"at half-past one in the morning."

Defiantly he said, "I'll be damned if I'm going to tell you."

"And you'll be damned if you don't," she reminded him.

"A typical double-bind situation, I believe, but you don't have to rub it in." His voice was reproachful. "Look here, I don't suppose if I promised to leave the Clinic first thing in the morning, ever so discreetly—"

She ignored him; she had just seen that her jewelry case stood open on the desk. "Have you a gun?"

He looked actually offended. "Of course not."

"I think I'd rather see for myself if you're telling the truth. Do you mind keeping your hands up?"

"Of course I mind," he said snappishly. "Have I any choice?"

"None at all." She approached him gingerly, noticing for the first time his clothes, a startling contrast to his daytime costumes, being entirely and soberly black: black pullover, black slacks and black rubber-soled shoes. Patting him she found no gun but there was an oddly shaped bulge in his left pocket. "Out," she said sternly. "Empty it."

"A scandal's not going to help the Clinic," he warned her. "If I go quietly—if I swear to you—"

"Out," she told him.

He sighed. From his pocket he drew a small black object that looked like a truncated binocular. "One jeweler's glass," he said resignedly, and digging again he brought out her emerald pendant and two ruby necklaces. "The diamond pin dropped on the floor by the desk," he told her, and added bitterly, "I suppose you know that every damned one of these pieces—for which you can send me to prison for years—is a blasted fake?"

Mrs. Pollifax stared incredulously at the display and then lifted her glance to him accusingly. "But you're only a jewel thief!" she cried.

"What to you mean 'only'?"

"Why didn't you say so at once!" she demanded. "I thought—I can't tell you how relieved I am."

He backed away from her in astonishment. "Relieved? I don't think my hearing's been affected but you said *relieved?*"

"Yes, terribly. It makes *such* a difference." She crossed to the windows, closed the balcony door and drew the curtains, really pleased to discover that her instincts had been sound after all. "Are you what they call a cat burglar?"

He sank into a chair. "I've never really thought about it. God I wish I had a drink," he said with feeling.

"Why were you going to steal my jewels if you knew they were fakes?"

"If you must know, they're damned good fakes and there's a market for good fakes. Look here, are you going to call the police?"

She considered this thoughtfully and shook her head. "On the whole, I think it wiser not—provided, of course, that you return Lady Palisbury's diamond."

He gaped at her. "Good God, you're clairvoyant!"

"It's simply a matter of listening and putting things together," she told him reassuringly. "Lady Palisbury had lost her diamond and now I discover a professional second-story man on the premises. You *are* a professional, aren't you?"

"I was," he said bleakly. "Until tonight."

"So you've never been caught before! You must be very good then?"

"Oh, one of the best," he told her dryly. "God, I wish I had a drink."

"I'll get you one." She patted him on the arm and went to her suitcase from which she removed two envelopes of instant mix and a pair of paper cups. "I always like to travel prepared," she told him. "Excuse me a minute." She went into the bathroom, filled the cups with hot water and returned, stirring them with the handle of a toothbrush.

"*Cocoa?*" he said disbelievingly.

"It helps to settle the nerves," she told him, pulling up a chair tête-à-tête. "You do realize, of course, that stealing jewelry is dishonest."

He managed a feeble smile. "I'm surprised it's just occurred to you."

"Have you tried more conventional work?"

He shrugged. "On occasion, but never with zest. I'm afraid I like the danger. I especially enjoy working alone."

She considered this and nodded. She could appreciate his point. "It's been remunerative?"

"Rather." She received the flash of a smile. "I've managed to salt away a few choice pieces of real estate. Clothes of course are a huge expense, and I drive a Mercedes convertible." He sighed. "The thing is, it takes a damnable lot of money to be rich."

"Mmmm," she murmured, studying him. "There's no import business, either?"

He shook his head.

"And I don't suppose Robin Burke-Jones is your real name?"

"Sorry about that," he apologized. "Actually it's plain Robert Jones." He sighed. "It's taken a damned lot of work turning myself into Burke-Jones and I wish the hell you'd tell me what you're going to do about me."

"I'm thinking about that myself," she admitted. "For the moment I wish you'd tell me how you arrived at my balcony without any noise. The gravel—how did you keep it from crunching like popcorn under your feet?"

"With the proper equipment—in this case padded runners—it's no bother." His glance suddenly narrowed and his face changed. "Look here," he said, "there's something wrong about this. About you, I mean. Surely you ought to be in hysterics or tears over finding a burglar in your room? Most women would have screamed or gone into shock by now, and you should never *never* be sitting here plying me with cocoa and inquiring about my techniques."

"I am always interested in people who do things well," she said with dignity.

He put down his cup. "I don't believe it. You shouldn't have given me cocoa, it's bringing me to my senses. Those jewels being fake—" He scowled at her. "You're not in desperate straits, are you? I mean I could lend you a hundred pounds if you're in trouble." A thought struck him and he added politely, "Or give you them."

She laughed. "I'm really very touched, but thank you, no."

"You're not going to blackmail me, and you're not going to inform—"

Mrs. Pollifax put down her cup and said crisply, "On the contrary, I said nothing about not blackmailing you."

He drew in his breath sharply. "I see. Yes, it would be that, of course."

"I propose an agreement," she suggested. "Terms, shall we call them? I shall say nothing at all of tonight's events, and nothing of your—uh—career so long as I hear sometime tomorrow that Lady Palisbury has found her missing diamond."

"Those are your only terms?" He looked taken aback.

"Almost. Have you robbed any other people here as well?"

He shook his head. "It's not my technique. I never commit myself until just before I'm ready to leave a place—it's too dangerous—but by that time I know precisely who to rob and how. I do my rehearsing ahead of time," he admitted. "Like tonight. As a matter of fact I've spent the last three nights out on the roofs—"

"Roofs!" she exclaimed.

"Yes, testing exits and entrances and generally getting the lay of the land. If you must know," he went on, "I overheard you telling the night porter a few hours ago that you had emeralds to put in the safe. Your voice carried, and I was in the solarium. I decided I'd better pay a visit ahead of schedule and see what you have. Most people don't bother with safes, they never believe anything will happen to their jewels."

This had the ring of truth. "And Lady Palisbury?"

He sighed. "No sense of property, that woman. She left her diamond out on her balcony two nights ago. Simply left it on the table." He shook his head disapprovingly. "Not even sporting of her. I ask you, what was a man to do?"

"Yes, I can see the temptation," said Mrs. Pollifax, nodding. "Tell me, how did you happen to choose this particular profession?"

"Is this part of the deal?" he asked darkly.

"No, but I'm terribly curious," she confided. "I'd feel so much more satisfied knowing."

He made a face. "There's no point in going into it, it's an extremely dull and vulgar story."

"But I enjoy dull and vulgar stories," she told him.

He shrugged distastefully. "If you insist, then. To be perfectly blunt about it, my name is not only *not* Burke-Jones but my father was a locksmith. Soho in London. Oh, very low caste," he said with a scowl. "As the eldest of six children—I can't possibly describe the accent I spoke with, the English very properly say that speech is breeding—my father taught me his trade so that by the time I was fifteen I could pick a mean lock." He sighed. "He went crooked just once, my father. For the sake of the money and God knows he needed it. Somebody offered him a small fortune to open a safe and—well, he was caught and died in jail. Of grief, I think. And that, dear lady, stirred in me a hatred of all 'systems'—that an honest trade brought debts and one fall from grace brought death and ruin."

"Life isn't fair, no," she agreed. "So it's anger that motivated you?"

"A very typical juvenile anger," he admitted, "but serving its purpose. I left school, totted up my assets—negligible—and decided to change myself. Went to acting school. No Oxford or Eton for me. No Hamlet, either. Acting school trimmed off the rough edges, put the h's back in my speech and removed the accent. Then I went off to the Riviera in borrowed clothes and made my first heist. But you see by the time the anger wore off I was too damned good at my trade to do anything else. There's nothing else I *can* do."

"Overspecialization," said Mrs. Pollifax, nodding sympathetically.

"A certain amount of hedonism, too," he admitted.

"I have often thought," she said idly, "that police and criminals have a great deal in common, the only difference being that they're on opposite sides of the law."

"Rather a large difference," he pointed out dryly.

She shook her head. "Purely one of intention, I'm sure. Both live by wit and deduction, don't they, and share a common isolation? It's always struck me that Sherlock Holmes took far more pleasure in talking to Professor Moriarty than to Doctor Watson."

He gave her a quizzical glance. "You've rather an unusual way of looking at things, haven't you?"

"I'm only thinking that you have invaluable talents," she told him thoughtfully.

He glanced at the clock on her night table. "Which I'd jolly well better put to work if I'm going to get Lady Palisbury's diamond back before dawn. You're really not going to call the police?"

She shook her head.

"And you'll let me—just walk out of this room?"

"You may consider yourself a free man."

He held out his hand and grinned at her. "I say, this has really been awfully pleasant. A bit strange but pleasant."

"It has," agreed Mrs. Pollifax, getting to her feet and beaming at him. "Actually it's been delightful. Which door will you leave by?"

"I'll feel much more secure leaving the way I came," he

assured her. "And look, if I can ever do anything for you in return—my room's directly above yours, number 213."

"Number 213," she repeated, and watched him vanish over the railing of her balcony. Although she listened very closely she could hear nothing, not even a whisper of gravel. A fantastic performance, she thought, and as she turned off her light—there seemed no point in bothering with locks again—she reflected that Robin could prove to be something of a jewel himself.

Eight

In the morning there was a doctor, a large, hearty man named Dr. Lichtenstein. While he poked and prodded her they made polite conversation about America; Mrs. Pollifax obligingly coughed for him and he poked and prodded her still more. "Very good," he said at last, and prescribed a metabolism test, a lung X-ray, three blood tests, and an electrocardiogram.

"All this for Hong Kong flu?" she protested.

"At your age," he hinted delicately, and then, shrugging, "Why else are you here?"

Mrs. Pollifax sensibly did not reply to this but it was exasperating to say the least. She repressed her crossness, however. She was waiting to ask him a question.

"In the meantime," he concluded, removing his stethoscope and placing it in his bag, "enjoy Montbrison. Walk in the gardens. Feel free to visit St. Gingolph, and over at Montreux there is the Castle Chillon, where Byron visited." He closed his bag and stood up, saying to the nurse, "You will please schedule the tests?"

Mrs. Pollifax also stood. "By the way," she said casually, "you are certainly the one person who can tell me how Madame Parviz is today. She wasn't well enough last night to see me." When the doctor looked blank she said, "Hafez's grandmother."

"Hafez?" he repeated, and turned to the nurse, who explained the question to him in French.

"Oh, the Zabyan group," said the doctor. "I know nothing about it, Madame Pollifax, they bring with them their own doctor."

Mrs. Pollifax sat down in astonishment. "You allow that? Isn't it very unusual?"

"Of this I do not approve," he admitted with a shrug. "But it happens sometimes, it happens. In a Clinic like this certain adjustments are made, you understand? It is handled entirely by the Board of Directors."

"You don't know why they're here, then?"

He turned with his hand on the doorknob. "I understand the woman is very old, very tired, she wishes to see Switzerland again but with no wish to be examined by foreign doctors. Good day, madame."

She nodded, scarcely aware of his departure. But this was very peculiar, she thought, frowning, and his statement, added to the reception given her last night by the Zabyans, threw an entirely different light on the situation. If no one ever saw the woman—"I *must* talk to Marcel," she realized, and picked up the phone to order her breakfast.

But when her breakfast arrived it was brought by a young apprentice waiter. Marcel, he said, was on late duty today and would not be in until after lunch. This was frustrating news, and Mrs. Pollifax found herself very cross about the odd communication system set up by Interpol. Still, she knew the hours Marcel kept, having seen him here at midnight. There was nothing to do but wait.

She breakfasted on her balcony, only a little charmed today by the birds and the stillness. After breakfast she went down to the garden to sit in the sun.

"I was utterly taken aback," said Lady Palisbury, speaking to Court. They stood on the graveled path and her voice carried across the flower beds. "We breakfasted on the balcony as usual, John and I, and John had no sooner sat down in his chair when he winced and jumped up again. He said he felt as if he'd sat on a golf ball. And there it was, my diamond, buried where the two chair cushions met. It had been there all the time!"

"Oh, Lady Palisbury, I'm so glad for you."

"My dear, you have no idea how glad I am for myself. John gave me that ring in 1940—"

Several feet away, ensconced in the sun, Robin turned to Mrs. Pollifax and murmured, "I'm actually blushing. It's downright embarrassing being such a benefactor."

Mrs. Pollifax smiled. "Painful, too, I should imagine. A good deed shining in a dark world—"

He groaned. "Please—spare me your clichés. and *don't* try to reform me."

Mrs. Pollifax followed his gaze to Court, whose long, straight brown hair gleamed in the sun. She looked remarkably wholesome and healthy, her bright pink dress emphasizing her sun-tanned face, and Robin's eyes were fixed upon her with hunger. "I may not have to," she said with a smile. Beyond Court the doors swung open and a nurse pushed out the man in the wheelchair. She thought idly what a shuttered face he had, a cruel one, too. She had never felt that suffering necessarily ennobled people; it could but more frequently it didn't. It depended on attitude. "But I notice that you didn't pack up and bolt this morning," she reminded Robin, "and you're actually out of bed before noon."

"I decided to stay on a few days. You know, have a vacation—like honest people?" He succeeded in wresting his gaze from Court and flashed a wicked grin at Mrs. Pollifax. "Besides, if you leave the Clinic first—if I outstay you—"

"It was a particularly virulent strain of flu," she reminded him.

"About that flu," he said. "It reminds me that after I left you last night I began remembering things. That jewelry case of yours, for instance. I didn't pick it up but I pushed it across the desk and I've never known a jewelry case to weigh so much. About ten pounds, I'd say."

"Perhaps that's where I keep my genuine jewelry," she told him pleasantly.

Court was moving toward them across the lawn and Robin jumped to his feet. "Miss van Roelen," he said happily. "I was wondering if you'd care to join me in a walk to the village before lunch."

Court looked at him with steady blue eyes. She hesitated and turned to Mrs. Pollifax. "I'd like to very much. The three of us?"

Mrs. Pollifax shook her head. "I'm having tests this morning."

Court glanced helplessly at Robin and Mrs. Pollifax realized that she was actually very shy. She wondered, too, if the girl hadn't sustained a few inner wounds recently that left her frightened of men. "But I'd certainly appreciate your bringing back four postcards for me," she said briskly. "It would be so terribly kind of you."

Court looked relieved and persuaded. "Of course," she said warmly. "Of course I will. Shall we go then?"

"Four postcards," Robin said gravely. He positively glowed with chivalry as he led her across the lawn, and Mrs. Pollifax, who had no need at all of postcards, saw them go with a sense of satisfaction. She began to look around the garden for Hafez but he had not appeared yet, and her roving glance caught the eye of the general sitting across the path from her and leaning on his cane. He bowed courteously.

"Good morning," she called.

His reply was too low for her to hear, and she left her chair for the empty one beside him. "Mrs. Pollifax," she told him, extending her hand.

"General d'Estaing, madame." His hand was dry and warm.

"A beautiful morning. You are feeling well today?"

He had surprising eyes in his strong pale face. They had remained alive and now they twinkled shrewdly in his lined face. "That is not a logical question to ask a very old man, madame. I have survived another day, that is all, neither triumphant nor particularly moved by the fact. I am, after all, eighty-nine."

"Eighty-nine!" exclaimed Mrs. Pollifax.

"The particular problem of being eighty-nine," he continued, "is that one has time to reflect upon a well-lived life but no friends with which to share the sweep of perspective. Have you ever come near to death, madame?"

"Yes," she said, nodding. "Near enough."

"Then you know that its terrors are exaggerated," he said simply.

"I think I should mind the waiting," she told him thoughtfully. "It must be rather like the last months of pregnancy, with no possible way to back out or change one's mind."

"You mean the irrevocability," he said, smiling. "Birth and death—no, we've no choice there." His gaze looked out upon the garden reflectively. "These young people, I find it ironic that they are learning how to live while I am learning how to die."

"Do you wish you could tell them how to live?"

He chuckled. "One cannot tell the young anything, madame."

She laughed. "Very true. General, in your work—I hear that you were head of the Sûreté—you learned a great deal about human nature?"

"Too much," he said dryly.

She hesitated. "You have met, perhaps, with real evil?"

"Evil," he mused, and she saw his eyes flash beneath the heavy brows. "You ask a Frenchman that, madame? I had the interesting experience once of meeting Hitler—"

"Ah," she breathed.

He nodded. "He impressed me, madame—this man who sent millions of Jews to their death and changed the course of history—with his ordinariness. Success encouraged his madness, of course, but that was the thing, you see: he was so ordinary. This is what astonished and alarmed me, that evil can be so commonplace. It is not in the face or in the words but in the heart, in the intentions. In my experience I have found only one form of evil to leave its visible mark."

"And what is that?"

"In general the act of murder leaves no mark on a man but I have found this is not true of the professional killer who murders more than once, and in cold blood. It is a curious fact that it shows in the eyes, madame, which I believe the poets call the windows of the soul. I have found the eyes of the habitual murderer to be completely empty. An interesting revenge by Nature, is it not?"

"Indeed yes," she murmured.

"The soul can be annihilated, you see—one must not trifle with it." He glanced at the nurse who had entered the garden bearing a tray of medicines and when she headed toward them he sighed. "Just as I thought, the medicine is for me. They must try to keep me alive a little longer, madame."

The nurse addressed him in French and they exchanged a few jokes before her eyes fell on Mrs. Pollifax. "Oh, but madame," she cried, "you are the one they search for, it is time for the tests. You go, eh?"

Mrs. Pollifax bid the general a good morning, and went.

After lunch Mrs. Pollifax stationed herself in the garden

to wait for Marcel. She chose the gazebo, because it was secluded and discouraged company, and she fortified herself with a paperback novel and a discarded *International Herald Tribune* that she had found in the library. The sun grew hotter and the shadows longer. Two of the younger waiters appeared and moved among the guests, taking orders, but it was a long time before Marcel appeared. When she saw him she stood up and waved. "Oh, *garçon!*" she called, summoning her newest French word.

Marcel made his way cautiously toward her, his eyes wary. "*Oui,* madame?"

With a smile pinned on her lips, and speaking through clenched teeth she said, "Are you a good actor, Marcel? I have to talk to you."

He grinned. "All Frenchmen are actors, madame." He unfurled an order pad and held a pencil poised above it. "Now madame. I shall smile, you shall smile, and we can speak."

"It's Madame Parviz again, Marcel. Have you any information yet?"

"It was requested last night by phone, when I returned to the village, but the information will have to come from Zabya. There should be something by tomorrow morning."

She nodded. "But there's more, Marcel. Did you know that none of the doctors have visited or examined her?"

He looked surprised. "This I did not know."

"Dr. Lichtenstein told me. I asked. He said it was cleared by the Board of Directors, and he explained it by saying that Madame Parviz—or so he was told—is very old and wants no foreign doctors examining her. But she isn't that old, Marcel, I saw her."

He looked doubtful. "Madame, I do not wish to be tactless but are you forgetting what we are here for? An invalid woman and a child, it seems most unlikely that they are involved—"

"Of course they're not," she said impatiently, "but there is something very peculiar there. Can you get me a list of the Board of Directors?"

He shrugged. "I have this already in my files, of course."

"I'm also curious, Marcel, about the man in the room across the hall from Madame Parviz. I should have asked you about him last night. He's in a wheelchair, I see him in the garden and in the dining room. I'm wondering if he isn't a member of their party, too."

Marcel sighed. "I can assure you that he is not, madame, because he did not arrive with them, he has been here for some time. Nor is he Zabyan." He frowned. "Room number 153 . . ." He shook his head. "I do not remember his name without referring to my list but I can find out his name in half an hour."

"I'd appreciate it if you could find out a great deal more."

He looked at her and smiled. Perhaps he found her amusing. "Very well, madame, I will do very thorough detective work on this man and by tonight I will have information for you, okay? But I would prefer better to hear something of Robin Burke-Jones, of whom I am most suspicious."

"And rightly so," she said, smiling back at him. "Actually I can tell you a great deal about him, almost all of it, I think, reassuring. He's—" She paused. Over Marcel's shoulder she saw Robin making his way across the lawn to her. "So if you'll make it crumpets with tea," she said in a normal voice.

He leaned foward. "I go off duty at midnight, madame. Can you meet me on the ground floor at that hour, by the elevator?"

"I'll be there. And lemon with the tea," she added, lifting her voice.

"And you can bring me a Scotch and soda," said Robin, collapsing into the chair beside hers. "Do you know that walking is strictly for the birds?"

"They fly," pointed out Mrs. Pollifax. "Are you just getting back from the village?"

He nodded. "We lunched there. *I* have returned but not Court. Oh no, she's still playing the organ in that old Anglican church by the café." He shuddered. "The organ, for heaven's sake."

"But how charming," said Mrs. Pollifax, smiling at him. "What a gifted person she must be. What in particular bothers you about that?"

"What bothers me is that she doesn't even know I *left*." In his indignation he was virtually gargling his words. "We stopped in the church on the way back, and the rector, or whoever he was, made conversation with us about the age of the church and its flying buttresses and then about music, and Court said she played and he begged her to try their new organ. She forgot about me," he concluded in a strangled voice.

Mrs. Pollifax nodded. "Yes, I thought you might find that a problem but I hoped not. She strikes me as being quite self-sufficient, you know." In the silence that followed she added tranquilly, "I've heard it makes for the very best marriages, actually."

"What does?" he asked suspiciously. "Organ music?"

"Self-sufficiency. So many marriages are parasitic, don't you think? The one party living through the other. Such a tragic waste of potential."

He regarded her with exasperation. "Look, I'm not planning to marry her or anyone. In my profession can you even imagine the complication of a wife? All I ask is a decent show of interest. I've got money, I'm not bad looking, I've been around—"

Mrs. Pollifax nodded. "Ego."

To her surprise he said humbly, "You really think it's that?"

"Yes, I do. You're quite accustomed to having your own way, I imagine. Especially with women, isn't that true?"

"I suppose so," he admitted forlornly.

"What draws you to Court, if I may be so presumptuous?"

"I've never met anyone *more* presumptuous." He hesitated as Marcel brought them drinks on a tray, removed them to the table and withdrew. "She's different," Robin said scowling. "She's little. Small, I mean. And cool but warm underneath. She needs caring for, you can see that at once."

"Oh at once," agreed Mrs. Pollifax gravely.

"But she doesn't realize that. There's a vulnerability about her—" He caught himself up, frowned and said briskly, "Of course she's impossible. Do you realize that for the first eight days of her stay here she left her bed at five-thirty in the morning to *walk*? The girl's obsessed, it's unnatural."

Mrs. Pollifax considered him with sympathy. "There are people like that, you know. My neighbor at home, Miss Hartshorne, is one." She said thoughtfully, "I think it arouses guilt feelings in the rest of us. Certainly Miss Hartshorne's not very popular but," she added loyally, "she's ever so healthy."

"Exactly," said Robin. "And you called her Miss Hartshorne. She never married?"

Mrs. Pollifax shook her head.

"Well then, you see?" He was triumphant. "That's just what will happen to Court. She's beautiful—breathtakingly lovely—and she'll never marry."

Mrs. Pollifax beamed at him happily. "Then you needn't worry about falling in love with her, need you? She's no threat at all."

"But you were in your room all day?"

"Oh, that is nothing *now*. Look, madame, the picture is going to begin. I will translate."

He did indeed translate; he read aloud to her even the credits on the screen, and then as the story began he faithfully recorded every word. It did not make him popular with the handful of other people present, among them Ibrahim Sabry and the Palisburys. Mrs. Pollifax leaned over and suggested he lower his voice. "Oh, *oui*, madame," he said, and for two minutes he did. Mrs. Pollifax decided the only way to restore tranquillity to the group was to withdraw. It was nearing her Flashlight Hour, anyway.

"You can tell me the plot tomorrow, I'm going to leave now," she whispered to him.

His disappointment was huge, but glancing back from the door she noted that it was fleeting. He was once again immersed in the show, eyes round, lips parted. She smiled at his enthrallment. It was good to see him a child again. Court and Robin were sitting in the library talking, their heads close together; she waved at them and went upstairs.

At ten o'clock, and feeling rather like Paul Revere, she went again to her balcony to signal that she had survived a second day at Montbrison. Again the car lights flicked on in reply and again she watched her unknown friend disappear down the hill. Still she lingered; it was warm this evening, with a feel of rain in the air. The lights along the shore of Lake Geneva were gauzy, like smudged yellow fingerprints on a dark canvas. She realized that she still had not seen the mountains that rimmed the lake.

At 11:55, after practising her Yoga for half an hour, she checked the scintillator counter and tested her flashlight and prepared to learn what Marcel might have discovered. Closing her door behind her she moved softly down the stairs. Again the concierge's station was abandoned; the elevator idled there, brightly lighted and empty. She descended to the ground floor. Marcel had not arrived yet but it still lacked a minute to the hour.

It was awkward waiting here by the elevator in the brightly lighted hall. The doors to the garden stood across the lobby opposite her, two rectangles of opaque black glass shining like eyes. She felt extremely conspicuous. The ground floor was quiet except for the sound of water running in the Unterwasser Massage room next to the garden doors. There was no whistling tonight from the kitchen, which she would explore once she left Marcel. She moved away from the staircase toward the shadows behind it, and the movement was reflected in the glass doors, a pale wraith mocking her with perfect synchronization.

She checked her watch; it was precisely midnight. The running water was annoying because someone would be coming back soon to turn it off and she could not imagine how she would explain her presence. The sound was insidious, like two gossips murmuring and whispering in another room. Otherwise the Clinic was silent and there was in this, too, an odd quality of restiveness. There was no sign of Marcel.

In the Unterwasser Massage room something dropped to the floor and Mrs. Pollifax stopped pacing and became still. An object had fallen but objects did not drop by themselves. She placed the jewel case in the shadow of the stairway and moved across the lobby to the door of the Unterwasser Massage room. There she hesitated, listening, and then turned the knob. The room was in darkness; she switched on her flashlight as she entered. Across from her the door that had led to Hydrotherapies was just closing. Its latch clicked softly and she saw the knob released from the other side by an unseen hand. She opened her mouth to call out but as she stepped forward the beam of her flashlight dropped and she gasped in horror.

Marcel lay in the pale green tub, his eyes turned vacantly to the ceiling. Blood spattered the sides of the tub and ran in zigzag lines across his white jacket. His throat had been cut from ear to ear.

"Oh dear God," she whispered, like a prayer, and sagged against the wall. Turning off her flashlight she groped for a chair and sat down and gulped in deep breaths of air. He could not have been dead for long, perhaps only seconds before she had descended the stairs. While she had been hurrying down to meet him here there had been stealthy movements in the dark, small animal sounds and sudden death. There had not even been time for him to call out.

The water still gurgled obscenely into the tub. After a moment—driven by a stern sense of duty—she switched on the flashlight again and crept back to Marcel. One trembling hand moved to his bloody jacket and waited but there was no flutter of a heartbeat, no possibility of survival. She rinsed the blood from her hand under the faucet and then found the spigot and angrily stilled the water.

At once she knew that she had made a dangerous mistake.

Her mind was clearing. Marcel was dead—murdered—and someone had left this room as she entered it.

She switched off the flashlight and stood up. The darkness was engulfing, and with the cessation of running water the silence proved to be as taut and alive as a scream. Somewhere in the three offices that lay between her and the Hydrotherapies room this silence was shared by another human being. Someone else listened to the emptiness and knew he wasn't alone: she had just told him so by turning off the water.

Marcel's murderer.

She stood irresolute. Into the silence there crept the faintest stirring of movement in the next room, a whisper of cloth against cloth, of protesting floorboards. He was returning. Marcel's murderer was coming back to see who was here.

She shivered. She did not believe she had been seen or

heard earlier. She had come downstairs silently. The stairs were heavily carpeted and on her feet she wore the heavy knitted bedsocks that Miss Hartshone tirelessly made for her every Christmas. She doubted that he even realized she had entered the room as he left it, but certainly he had heard the water stop splashing into the tub. He was coming back to learn who was here, and a little knowledge was a dangerous thing. For her.

She looked around her. She was isolated in this small room next to the brightly lighted lobby. Behind the murderer, on the other hand, lay three offices and a gymnasium-size room, giving him considerable space in which to move about and hide. Apparently his curiosity outweighed his caution and he felt impelled to search and to identify. She did not care to explore the reasons behind his logic because if he discovered her, then she discovered him as well. She did not believe he would accept such mutuality.

She must not be found here.

Quietly she backed to the door by which she had entered the room. She opened it and assessed the distance across the lobby to the staircase. Impossible, in such a bright light he would clearly see her before she gained the stairs. She turned back and pointed her flashlight at the door across the room, waiting for him to enter. A very small idea had occurred to her.

Slowly the knob began to turn. Matching her movement to his she left as he entered, fleeing into the hall—but not to the stairs, she rushed headlong to the utility room around the corner and flung herself inside. There she ran her flashlight over the fuseboxes: they were labeled in French, in English, and by number. She tugged at the circuit-breakers for the ground floor and a second later saw the light under the closed door vanish.

The silence was frightening. A door closed. Footsteps moved across the lobby to the foot of the stairs, and for that moment the two of them were separated only by the wall of the closet. She held her breath. He would be holding his breath, too, she thought, scarcely daring to expel it lest he miss some small, stifled sound. He was going to begin stalking her now like prey in an attempt to rush her out of hiding. And while they both waited, their thoughts screaming in the emptiness, he moved again.

He walked past the closet and down the hall toward the gymnasium, giving her just one fragile unguarded moment of hope. When she heard the doors to Hydrotherapies swing open she slipped out of the closet and raced to the stairs, snatching up the scintillator counter from the floor where she had left it.

When she reached the Reception floor level her heart was thudding ominously and her throat ached from dryness. She felt almost sick with horror. She stopped to catch her breath and saw the elevator still idle; on impulse she entered it. For a second she hesitated over the panel and then she punched the button for the floor above her own. *He must not learn which floor was hers.*

But he had heard the sound of the elevator in motion, for as she ascended with frustrating slowness she recognized the sound of feet pounding up the stairs below her. She realized he was racing up to cut her off, and his determination to find and identify her was terrifying. Slowly the elevator rose toward the fourth floor and slowly the doors opened. She stepped out. Another moment and she would be trapped unless—

Robin, she thought. Robin had said he was in the room exactly above hers. She ran down the hall, found room 213, discovered the door unlocked and stumbled inside.

Robin was sitting up in bed with a book on his knees. He looked at her in astonishment. "My dear Mrs. Pollifax," he said, and then seeing her face he gasped, "My God, what on earth?"

She shook her head, placed a finger to her lips and retreated into the darkness of his bathroom. There were advantages in appealing to a cat burglar; Robin responded at once by reaching for his bedside lamp and plunging the room into darkness. In silence they listened to footsteps walking down the hall toward the solarium. Softly the footsteps returned. After a short interval the elevator doors slid closed and the elevator hummed as it descended.

Slowly Mrs. Pollifax expelled her caught breath.

Robin went to the door and opened it, looked up and down the corridor and then closed and locked the door and walked across the room to draw the curtains of the window. Turning on a light he said pleasantly, "We're having a party in my room tonight?"

She left the darkness of his bathroom and found him rummaging in his wardrobe closet. "There's a bottle of Napoleon brandy here somewhere," he said. "Ah, here we are. Beautiful. I have never felt that cocoa measures up to brandy in a crisis." He poured an inch into a bedside glass and handed it to her. "Drink it down, you look like hell."

She nodded gratefully.

"And while you're thawing out," he continued pleasantly, "you'll no doubt think up some outrageous lie to explain why you've been playing hide-and-seek with someone in the halls at this ungodly hour, but don't—don't try —because I won't believe you. When you stumble into a man's room in the middle of the night, looking as if you'd just seen a corpse, and carrying of all things that damn jewelry case—" His eyes narrowed as he sprang to his feet.

"Robin!" she cried sharply.

He picked up the box and carried it to the light. "Sorry, milady," he said. "Curiosity killed the cat but never a cat burglar, as you call it. I've been curious about this thing all day, and obviously you're not what you appear to be. Let's see what you really are." She sat mute as he opened the case. "Let's see, if I designed this—oh, it's very well done—I'd put the lock in one of these hinges, I think, and—" He triumphantly pressed the hinge on the right and removed the tray.

There was silence as he peered down at what he'd unearthed. "Good God, *not* the Queen's jewels. A—surely not a *Geiger* counter?" He stared at her disbelievingly.

She sighed and put down the emptied glass of brandy. "As a matter of fact, yes. Did you really expect stolen goods?"

He looked bewildered. "I don't know, I expected something illicit, although you don't *look* illicit. But a Geiger counter? What on earth are you looking for, uranium?" He thought he was making a joke.

Mrs. Pollifax considered him, hesitated and then made a decision. "Plutonium, actually."

"Plutonium?"

"Yes." There was a welcome impersonality about plutonium. It did not bleed, it was a metallic object without hopes, dreams, fears, or a throat that could be cut. At the moment plutonium seemed much less dangerous than Marcel's body lying in the Unterwasser Massage tub, and she did not want to speak of Marcel. She had sought sanctuary in this room, and Robin had saved her from being discovered and possibly killed. For this she owed him something, even truth, but if Robin was to be involved then let him be involved in an abstract without personality. Marcel's murder was too dangerous to share.

"Interpol is in this," she told him gravely, "and my government is in this, and yours, too."

He shuddered. "That's a bit thick." He stared ruefully at the scintillator counter in his lap. "My God, I've opened Pandora's box, haven't I? You're involved with my mortal enemies and I'm sitting here listening to you." He shook his head. "Damn it, I wish I'd allowed you to think up that outrageous lie."

"You didn't give me time," she reminded him.

"Plutonium . . . It would have to be stolen plutonium, of course."

"Yes. Presumed to have been sent here."

"Pretty damned clever sending it *here*." He began to look interested. "Not a bad drop-off point at all. I don't have to ask what your precious authorities are afraid of, of course, but they're not going to relish your telling me this, are they? Why did you?"

She thought about this a moment, a little startled herself at her openness. "I find no evil in you," she said at last, very simply. "It's true that you have a somewhat distorted sense of morality in one area but I'm looking for someone with no morality at all. Someone"—she shivered—"completely amoral, without scruples or fear or compassion or decency."

"Here?" he said in astonishment. "Among the patients?"

"Perhaps."

He looked at her. "So that's why you were relieved to find me only a thief. And tonight? What did you find tonight? Who was it out there?"

"I wish I knew. I wish I'd had the cunning to find out." The memory of Marcel intervened and she steadied herself. When she replied it was casually. "I was downstairs on the ground floor when I found myself playing cat-and-mouse with someone in the dark. I reached the Reception floor and the elevator was standing there and so I slipped inside, planning to walk down a floor to my room, you see, but I could hear whoever it was running upstairs after me, so I was cut off and—"

"And popped in here." He studied her face shrewdly. "If that's your story I won't do any more prying, but to be perfectly frank with you that little anecdote doesn't begin to match the look on your face when you burst into my room. Do you think whoever it was is still out there waiting for you?"

He had caught her off guard; she realized that she'd not thought of this yet.

Robin shook his head. "You don't have a poker face tonight, Mrs. Pollifax, I frightened you with that question." He regarded her curiously. "All right, I said I wouldn't pry but let's proceed as if you've stolen the Queen's jewels and the police are lurking. Can you manage a drop of eight feet on a rope?"

She brightened. "Over the balcony?"

He looked amused. "Yes, my dear Mrs. Pollifax, but don't look so eager. Have you ever before gone up or down a rope?"

"Yes, once in Albania—" She stopped. "Oh dear, I *am* tired, I should never have said that."

He looked her up and then down, taking in her height, her weight, her flyaway hair, the voluminous robe and woolly bedsocks, and he grinned. "I didn't hear you say it. I wouldn't believe it if I did hear it, especially knowing that Americans are not allowed in Albania. Who would believe it anyway, I ask you." He removed a coil of efficient-looking rope from his suitcase. "Mountain climbing rope," he explained, patting it lovingly. "The very best. By the way, there's nothing to this, there's no ledge at all on this floor but a perfectly splendid one on yours below so there'll be something under you all the way. I'll go first and check you out." Over the coil of rope he studied her and frowned. "You know, it terrifies me discovering who you are, but it's equally alarming to think your superiors may have sent you here alone and unprotected. I daresay it's the most absolute affrontery to offer my services but if anything comes up—" He looked embarrassed. "Well, hang it all, I'm already indebted to you, and if you should need a gentleman burglar—"

"I can't tell you how much I appreciate that," she said warmly.

"Oh?" He looked startled. "Well, do keep it in mind,

then. By the way, is your balcony door locked?" She nodded and he added a circle of keys to his belt. "Full speed ahead then." On the balcony he tied the rope to the railing, fussed over the knots, tested the railing and glanced up. "All set?"

It was dismayingly dark out here but she reflected that this had the advantage of blotting out the garden four stories below. "I'm ready."

"Good. Give me your jewelry case. Once over the railing lean out a bit, rope in hand, and then slide down and *in.*"

"In," she repeated.

He disappeared and Mrs. Pollifax found herself hesitating until she remembered the lighted halls and the shadowy solariums where anyone could hide. She climbed over the railing and grasped the rope. Closing her eyes she murmured a brief prayer and let go.

"Good girl," said Robin, catching the rope and guiding her in close to the balcony. "With a little training you'd make a splendid burglar." He helped her over the railing, turned his pencil-thin flashlight on the door to her room and a moment later it stood open. "I trust you locked your other door, the one into the hall?"

She shook her head. "No, I thought I might have to retreat in a hurry."

"Then I'd better take a look around and make sure nobody else used it for a hasty retreat." He followed her inside and while she put away the scintillator counter he glanced under her bed, into her closet and then disappeared into the bathroom. She heard him swear softly and then he sputtered angrily, "What the devil!"

She turned questioningly toward the door just as he reappeared pushing a frightened Hafez in front of him. "Behind your bathtub curtain," he said grimly. *"Hiding."*

Ten

Hafez stood very still in front of her
but there was no quietness in him; he was taut with anxiety. He had been crying, of this there was no doubt, because his eyes were red-rimmed and his cheeks still damp. "Where have you been?" he cried despairingly. "I came to find you and you'd gone and I waited for you so long."

"Behind the shower curtain?" inquired Robin dryly.

"No, no, monsieur, in that chair over there—for fifteen minutes—but then I heard your voices on the balcony and I was afraid."

"But why?" asked Mrs. Pollifax softly. "Why aren't you in bed asleep?"

He hesitated, looking at Robin.

"I think you can regard him as a friend," Mrs. Pollifax told him.

Hafez looked doubtful.

"Try," begged Mrs. Pollifax.

"If you say so, madame," He turned back to her. "I have come to take you to my grandmama. She is awake now. Please," he urged, "you will come with me quickly?"

"At two o'clock in the morning!" exclaimed Mrs. Pollifax.

Robin said flatly, "Nonsense, lad, Mrs. Pollifax isn't going anywhere except to bed."

Watching Hafez, Mrs. Pollifax realized that she had heard of people turning white but she had never seen it happen before. The color literally drained from Hafez's face, as if his whole world depended upon her coming with him and Robin, as judge and jury, had turned down his appeal. She was touched and astonished. Rallying, she said, "On the contrary, it needn't take long." Turning to Robin she explained, "It's not as if his room is on another floor, it's just down the hall at the other end."

Robin said angrily, "Are you mad?"

"Probably."

He sat down in the chair by the desk and mutinously folded his arms. "Well, I'm staying right here, I'm not leaving until I see you settled for the night. Damn it, that's why I escorted you, remember?"

She gave him a forgiving glance. "I won't be long."

He added furiously, "If you're not back soon I'll turn the whole Clinic upside down. What's the room number?"

"It is 150, monsieur," said Hafez, regarding him with awe.

Robin nodded and Mrs. Pollifax gave him a last thoughtful glance as she gathered up her skirts. His attitude struck her as exaggerated, considering how little he knew about the events of her evening, and she wondered what caused it. "Let's go, Hafez," she said quietly, and heard him sigh with relief.

The hall was mercifully empty. Hafez tiptoed ahead of her and Mrs. Pollifax, who had only slightly recovered from her last venture into the halls, was happy to tiptoe with him. Down near the end of the hall Hafez stopped and drew a key from his pocket. Unlocking the door he beckoned her inside the dimly lit room. Somewhat nervously she stepped across the threshold and hesitated.

The normality of the scene reassured her. This time there was no Serafina, and the door to the adjoining rooms was closed. A small lamp burned at the night table, throwing shadows against the wall and a circle of light across the bed in which Madame Parviz sat braced against a number of pillows. She wore a rough homespun robe with a hood that shaded her face but even at a distance Mrs.

Pollifax could see an uncanny resemblance to Hafez. A pair of brilliant dark eyes watched her approach; in the dim light they glittered under deeply cut lids but as Mrs. Pollifax drew closer she was shocked to see dark shadows under the eyes, like bruises. It was a ravaged face, once exotic, still handsome but drained of all vitality now. Only the essence of a strong character remained, and a certain imperial air that she shared with her grandson.

"Grandmama," said Hafez quietly, "here is my friend Madame Pollifax."

"Enchanté," murmured the woman in a low voice, and one hand lifted to indicate the chair next to the bed. Her voice when she spoke was filled with exhausted pauses, as if a great effort was being made. "I understand you—paid me—a call yesterday. When I was—asleep."

"Yes, Hafez and I have become friends," said Mrs. Pollifax, smiling. "You've a very charming grandson, Madame Parviz, I've been enjoying him." Her own voice sounded alarmingly healthy and she lowered it.

Madame Parviz did not respond to the pleasantry; her eyes remained fixed upon Mrs. Pollifax with an intensity that was embarrassing. "May I—ask a favor, then, Mrs. —Pollifax?"

The abruptness was startling in a woman so obviously gracious. Mrs. Pollifax glanced at Hafez, standing at the foot of the bed, and saw that he was watching her with the same intentness. "But of course," she said, suddenly very still and alert. "Of course."

"If I may ask—one thing Hafez—cannot do. A cable—sent from the village?"

"A cable," repeated Mrs. Pollifax.

"Not from—the Clinic."

"I see," said Mrs. Pollifax, almost holding her breath now. "You'd like me to send a cable for you but not from the Clinic." Turning practical she reached for her purse. "I've pencil and paper. If you'll dictate what you'd like—"

Hafez said quickly, "It is already prepared, madame."

And this was true: from beneath her blanket Madame Parviz drew a sheet of Clinic stationery and offered it to Mrs. Pollifax. "Please—you will read it?"

The silence as Mrs. Pollifax accepted it was heavy with suspense and she realized it was because two of the three people in this room were holding their breath. The mood was contagious and she heard herself read it aloud in a low, conspiratorial whisper. "To General Mustafa Parviz, Villa Jasmine, Sharja, Zabya: HAFEZ AND I SAFE AND WELL LOVE ZIZI."

Having read it Mrs. Pollifax was struck by its normalcy and curious at its necessity. "But it's not to be telephoned from the Clinic," she repeated.

"Please—no."

From the adjoining room, behind the closed door, there came an abrupt human sound resembling a snore; it *was* a snore, decided Mrs. Pollifax, hearing the sound move down the scale and then repeat itself and she saw Hafez and his grandmother exchange a warning glance.

"Is something wrong?" asked Mrs. Pollifax quietly.

"Wrong?" Madame Parviz turned quickly toward her and produced a laugh that was high and unnatural. "But—of course not!" Having managed this she leaned back exhausted against the pillows. "But—of course not, madame," she echoed.

"She is tired," Hafez said in a low voice.

The audience had ended. "Yes," agreed Mrs. Pollifax and arose and moved with him to the door. There she stopped and looked at Hafez thoughtfully. "You and your grandmother are very close, Hafez."

He nodded. His eyes were wary.

On impulse she leaned over and kissed the top of his head. "I like you very much, Hafez, and I think you're an ingenious young man."

"I beg your pardon, madame?"

She shook her head. "Never mind. Good night, I'll go to my room now."

She walked down the empty hall and entered the sanctuary of her room with a sense of relief. Robin sat in the chair by the desk, arms still folded across his chest. "Well?" he said, glowering at her.

"Well," she said, taking a deep breath.

"You finally met the vampire grandmother? You're satisfied?" A close look at her face and he sighed. "All right, you're not satisfied."

"It's been—a strange night," she admitted.

"You're reckless," he said. "Good God but you're reckless. Upstairs you were frightened of the halls, pale as a ghost, and then thirty minutes later you're tootling off on impulse with a small boy whom *anybody* could have sent. Anybody."

"Yes," she said absently.

"I get the feeling you're not hearing me."

"It's just turned Sunday," put in Mrs. Pollifax, frowning. "Where can one send a cable on Sundays, Robin?"

He gestured toward the night table. "You pick up the telephone, and provided the night porter's at the desk, and providing he's the one who speaks English—"

She shook her head. "I mean where does one go to send one personally, from an office."

He sighed. "You'd have to go to Montreux for that, to a PTT building. The telegraph is open on Sundays—8:30, I think, closed most of the afternoon and open again in the evening. I'll take you down in my car if you'd like."

She gave him a skeptical glance. "At 8:30 in the morning?"

He climbed to his feet. "Yes, at 8:30." He studied her face a moment and then said quietly, "Suppose you meet me at eight beside my car, which is parked around the corner from the main entrance. It's a dark blue Mercedes convertible. Will you do that?"

"It's very kind of you," she said, surprised.

"Not at all." He paused with one hand on the knob of the door to the balcony. "It's certainly been interesting seeing how the other half lives—the respectable half," he added with irony. "Sleep well, milady."

"Thank you."

"Oh, and by the way," he added, "I'd advise your taking a close look at that robe of yours before you wear it again. There's rather a lot of blood on it in the back, as if you'd knelt in a puddle of the stuff."

She stared at him in astonishment.

"I didn't notice it when you first popped into my room but when I saw it I had a fair idea of what frightened you tonight, and frankly it scares the hell out of me. See you at eight." He went out, carefully closing the door to the balcony behind him.

Considerably jolted Mrs. Pollifax stared after him and then she moved to the door and locked it behind him. His remark explained the reason behind his sudden protectiveness—he *knew*. She took off the offending robe, eyed it wearily and dropped it to the floor. There was suddenly a great deal to do, and a great deal to think about, but she was exhausted. Setting her alarm clock for seven she fell across her bed and sank into a sleep interrupted only spasmodically by small Unterwasser nightmares.

Eleven

The next morning Mrs. Pollifax breakfasted in the dining room and discovered that at 7:15 she was the only patient to do so. She found no unusual activity on the Reception floor, and the waiter who served her gave no indication that one of his colleagues had met with violent death during the night. When she had finished her coffee she left and descended to the ground floor, ostensibly for a stroll in the garden but actually to see what had been happening in the Unterwasser Massage room.

She discovered to her surprise that nothing appeared to be happening at all. The halls were deserted and the door to the massage room stood open. She moved toward it cautiously and stopped on the threshold. Inside, the pale green tub gleamed spotlessly. Sunlight poured through the frosted windows, striking the faucets and dials with silver and illuminating an immaculate and freshly polished floor. There was not so much as a hint that only hours ago a murder had taken place here, and for just a moment Mrs. Pollifax wondered if she might be losing her mind and had dreamed the murder.

Odd, she thought, frowning, and found it strange that no police were on duty here. Very odd, she mused and went upstairs to see if any police could have taken refuge in the offices behind the switchboard. But the offices were shuttered and locked and although she leaned against the door and listened she could hear no voices. Certainly the discovery of a body in the Unterwasser Massage room was an embarrassment but at the moment the Clinic's discretion seemed excessive and inhuman.

"Madame?" said the porter, peering around the corner at her.

She opened her mouth to speak, closed it and shook her head. It was nearly eight o'clock; she went out to find Robin in the turnaround.

Nothing was said as Robin backed his car and drove it up the narrow entrance to the Clinic and along the ravine. Emerging from the woods into bright sunlight he maneuvered his dark blue Mercedes through the streets of the village and headed it down the mountain toward Villeneuve.

"This is extremely kind of you," Mrs. Pollifax said at last.

As if a few hours had never intervened he said harshly, "All right, whose blood was it?"

She had been expecting the question; it had stood like a wall between them ever since she had stepped into the car. "The waiter, Marcel's," she told him quietly.

Looking appalled, Robin braked the car and drew it to a stop by the side of the road. "Hurt or dead?"

"Dead."

"Good God, do you mean murdered?"

She studied his face and nodded. "Yes, in the Unterwasser Massage room, in the tub. Did you know him, Robin?"

"Damned right I knew Marcel, he waited on my table and we had a bet on today's French bicycle race." He sat staring at her incredulously. "You found him there dead and— Was that all, or was there really someone else down there?"

Remembering, she shivered. "As I went into the Unterwasser Massage room by one door someone was just leaving by the opposite door. I almost called out, but then I saw Marcel lying there in the tub, all bloody and—" Her voice broke and she steadied it. "Yes, there was someone else down there, and someone very curious about me."

"His murderer?"

"I think so, yes."

"Good God, were you seen?"

She shook her head. "I'm quite sure I wasn't." She added wryly, "You see, I'd been reconnoitering the basement just as you've been reconnoitering the roofs. I knew where the fuseboxes were and that, I suppose, is what saved me."

He slowly shook his head. "That was cutting it a bit thin. Good God! But look here, why on earth Marcel? Why would anyone go after a perfectly innocent waiter—"

A thought struck him and his eyes narrowed. "Or wasn't he a perfectly innocent waiter?"

"Actually he wasn't," she admitted. "He was an Interpol man looking for the same thing I am. Oddly enough you seemed to be his chief suspect."

Robin whistled through his teeth. "Good Lord, I hope you told him—no, I hope you didn't."

"I was going to tell him last night except—except—"

"Yes, *except*," he filled in grimly. "Well, at least they didn't send you here alone, which lifts my respect for your superiors a notch. Look here, I told you before if there's anything I can do to help—"

"You're helping now, Robin, and I appreciate it."

"You mean by taking you to the telegraph office." He nodded and eased the car out into traffic again. "This cable you're sending is for Hafez's grandmother, of course?"

She smiled. "How wasted you are on petty crime, Robin. Yes, it's for Madame Parviz. Would it be against your scruples to help me do some balcony spying on room 150 when it's dark tonight?"

"Against my scruples!" He laughed. "Bless you for being so delicate about it, my dear Mrs. P., I'd be delighted to do some spying with you. What exactly did you find in room 150 last night?"

"On the surface, nothing," she said soberly.

"Ah, but under the surface?"

"A great many undercurrents." She was silent, staring ahead of her as they entered Montreux and Robin threaded the car through quiet streets. "Madame Parviz looked very ill and she was still quite weak. She asked me to send a cable for her announcing their safe arrival, to a man with the same name in Zabya. A General Parviz."

"That sounds normal enough."

She nodded. "Yes, until one remembers that Hafez and his grandmother have been at the Clinic for a week, and that she insisted the cable *not* be sent from the Clinic. There were only the three of us in the room but someone was asleep in the adjoining one—again very normal considering the hour—but when the sound of a snore was heard through the walls both Madame Parviz and Hafez looked alarmed. There was a kind of—of hushed urgency about our meeting."

"You mean you had the impression no one must know you were there?"

"Exactly. I'm trying to be very clear in my thinking," she told him earnestly. "Hafez has been frightened ever since I first met him, and I've not wanted to exaggerate or be melodramatic but I've felt he was trying to tell me something. Not consciously, you understand, but with every gesture and every expression. He's an unusually intelligent child, and I think he's been trying desperately to—"

When she faltered Robin gave her a quick glance. "To what?"

"To cope," she said softly. "Cope with something quite beyond him. I've been getting little messages consistently, without a word spoken. It's what I've felt from the beginning." She hesitated, feeling for words. "Everything matters terribly to children, you know, they're fresh and unformed, but of course they can exaggerate, too, so I had to be sure. Now I'm finally beginning to understand."

He stopped the car and backed it into a parking space and Mrs. Pollifax saw that across the street a large building bore the sign PTT. "Understand what?" asked Robin, turning off the ignition.

"I think I'd better send the cable first," she said. "It's half-past eight?"

"Just."

Mrs. Pollifax nodded and climbed out of the car and crossed the street. Entering the echoing, cavernous room she went to the telegraph window and copied out Madame Parviz's message, hesitating only when she reached the space for the sender's name. Since privacy seemed to matter very much to Madame Parviz she stood a moment, reflecting, pencil in hand. Inspiration arrived at last and feeling quite resourceful at keeping the Clinic out of it she wrote the name of William Carstairs, The Legal Building, Baltimore, Maryland. With that accomplished she paid for it and left.

"You were beginning to understand something," said Robin when she rejoined him, "and I hope you're not going to leave me hanging in midair."

"Oh, that," she said. "Yes, I'm beginning to understand why it's been impossible for Hafez to tell me anything. He *can't*. I'm also beginning to understand to what lengths he went to arrange my visit last night with his grandmother. It wasn't easy."

Robin looked startled. "You're implying a great deal wrong indeed."

"Yes, I am. Can we go back now? I want to sit in the garden and think, preferably over a pot of very hot coffee."

He started up the car. "I've nothing against thinking. I don't suppose I should ask about what in particular?"

"About thirteen tablets of aspirin, and what I report at ten o'clock tonight when I make my rather primitive contact with Interpol, about Marcel's death and what I tell the police when they make their inquiries."

"Which explains everything and nothing but I've already learned enough to scare the hell out of me. I wish it would scare the hell out of you," he said with a sidelong glance at her face. "I think I'm going to keep a very close eye on you today if you don't mind."

"I don't mind at all," said Mrs. Pollifax imperturbably.

As they drove into the entrance road of the Clinic and past the greenhouse Mrs. Pollifax saw a man in a green apron sweeping the steps, and Hafez seated on the top stair with his chin in his hand, the very same scene that had met her glance when she arrived on Friday. Now it was Sunday and Marcel was dead. She thought it would have been very convenient on Friday to have been clairvoyant and to have seen the seeds of destruction waiting here for catalyzation. The workings of fate always struck her with awe, for on these small assignments she inevitably arrived just in time to meet the effect of causes sown recklessly long ago. Marcel had been sent here, and had died, and his death in turn was setting new influences in motion. Where it would lead she couldn't guess but she knew that at some point influences and coincidences would converge. Nothing, she felt, happened purely by accident; it was an unraveling process.

As she walked toward the door Hafez stood up, eyes anxious and inquiring. "It's been taken care of," she told him in a low voice.

"Oh, thank you, madame," he gasped. His hand reached out to touch her arm, trembled there a moment, and then he turned and ran off up the stairs.

"Where are you going now?" Robin demanded.

Amused, she said, "To my room first, to order some coffee for the garden and to put away my sweater, and then—"

"Okay," he said hastily, "I'll see you later."

He too went up the stairs but Mrs. Pollifax lingered, her glance moving over the head of the concierge to the office behind him. It was still empty. There were no secretaries, no directors, no police in plainclothes in consultation and she found herself uneasy.

"Madam is looking for someone?" asked the head concierge.

She shook her head.

"Perhaps madam would like a copy of yesterday's *Herald Tribune*," he suggested. "We were sent an extra paper."

She thanked him, tucked it under her arm and went upstairs. As she changed into a cooler dress she briefly scanned the front page of the *Tribune*. The Common Market had agreed upon new farm tariffs. The price of silver had hit an all-time high. A minor official had been assassinated in Syria. She turned a page and found a photograph of King Jarroud of Zabya, and because this was Hafez's king she ran her eyes down the column quickly while she zipped up her dress. On Tuesday the King was celebrating his fortieth birthday and his tenth year in power . . . A parade, lunch in the palace beside the beautiful Arabian Nights pool, America's vice-president among the long list of luminaries invited to the daylong festivity . . . Jarroud an extremely popular monarch with the people but not without his enemies, mainly among those of the upper class who distrusted his sweeping reforms . . . Had already done much to narrow the huge gap between rich and poor . . . Illiteracy rate reduced from 89 percent to 21 percent after ten years of compulsory schooling, 80 percent of the people now owned some land . . . the country 60 percent desert.

"Mmm," she murmured, postponing details until later, and moved to the telephone to order coffee sent to the garden. Really, this life of luxury was infectious and she wondered how she would ever adjust again to washing dishes.

Fifteen minutes later she descended to the ground floor and again strolled past the Unterwasser Massage room, hesitating only a moment when she found it still deserted. She understood very clearly that a murder could empty the rooms of any establishment in a matter of hours but it was unbelievable to her that no traces remained of an event that must have shaken the Clinic to its foundations. Did a man's life count for so little these days?

She pulled a chaise longue into the sun and lay down, recalling Marcel's dancing blue eyes and his mock, comic gestures. When death came to the general, she thought, it would be a completion, it would be the closing of a circle on a fulfilled life but there were the other deaths, the ones that did violence to meaning by their abrupt and senseless interruption of life, and it was these deaths she mourned in particular. Why had it been necessary to sentence Marcel to death? What had he done? Most vital of all, *what had he known?*

The general was being helped into a chair by the nurse. The Palisburys, she noticed, had already arrived and were establishing themselves under the poplar tree. The man in the wheelchair, Ibrahim Sabry, sat beside a table with a pink umbrella and read a thick newspaper. The same tableau was arranging itself but Marcel was missing. Fraser, too, had been snatched away from this tranquil garden scene and no one had missed him, just as few people would notice Marcel's absence. And someone among these people was a murderer . . . someone here *knew.*

The glass doors swung open and a white-jacketed waiter came out bearing a tray. Seeing her he crossed the lawn toward her, picking up a small table as he came. "*Bon jour,* madame—your coffee!" he said.

Marcel had brought her tea yesterday with just such a flourish but now he was dead and in his murder lay the answer to a good many things if only she could find the right question to ask. "Thank you," she said absently, and as the waiter left she went back in her thoughts to yesterday. She had hailed Marcel and asked him if he was a good actor. He had taken out his order book while she told him of her anxieties about Madame Parviz. He had not thought highly of them but he had agreed to look into them. And he had told her—just before Robin arrived— that he would have information for her at midnight.

He had been safe at that hour yesterday, she was sure of it.

She thought, Whatever Marcel did after I saw him in the afternoon must have taken him closer to something, turned him in a new and different direction, toward territory someone had marked off as forbidden. The question was, what had Marcel done between half-past three in the afternoon and midnight, when he was killed? Whatever Marcel had discovered she must discover, too.

"I hate to disturb your thinking processes," said Robin, strolling up behind her, "but I've been looking for Court and I can't find her anywhere. Has she passed this way?"

"My thinking processes are behaving very poorly at the moment," she said, "and no, I've not seen her. Would you care for a cup of coffee?"

"I'd love one if you have a spare." He pulled up a chair and sat down. "Look here, shouldn't there be an air of repressed alarm here today, a few damp eyes, a policeman or two? I can't help noticing that business is very much as usual."

"I've noticed it, too," she said, nodding. "It bothers me."

"Yes, I thought it might. Of course things are very different for the rich, you know. They've got to be protected and they pay liberally for that when they come here. They're not supposed to be exposed to anything viler than an enema. It makes life in such a place a complete conspiracy." He grinned cheerfully. "At the casinos they handle it very tidily, you know. A chap blows out his brains after losing his last shilling and three minutes later you can't even find traces of the blood. I should resent that very much if it were I, and come back at once to haunt them."

"You're being abominably flippant and you're not cheering me up at all," she told him.

"Well, then, I wish you'd—oops!" he said in a startled voice and ducked his head under the table.

Mrs. Pollifax looked behind her to see what had surprised him and saw walking across the lawn one of the handsomest men she had ever seen, which startled her, too, if for different-reasons. *Gilbert Roland,* she thought, and then chided herself for such sentimental nonsense. Ibrahim Sabry was looking up from his newspaper and smiling—yes, the stranger was heading for Sabry—but everyone in the garden was watching as well. The man was wearing a dark pin-striped business suit but this scarcely succeeded in scaling him down to life size. He was a figure out of an epic, tall, lean, proud, a beak of a nose set in a swarthy face, his eyes gleaming under straight quizzical brows, his smile a flash of white in his dark face. "Who," said Mrs. Pollifax with feeling, "is *that!*"

Robin slid back into his chair looking sheepish but she noticed that he moved his chair so that he could sit with his back to the newcomer. She, on the other hand, moved her chair so that she could watch the stranger shake hands with Sabry.

"Reflex action—sorry about that," confessed Robin. "I forget that people I've lifted a few jewels from really have no idea I'm the culprit. That's Yazdan Kashan. Good Lord, I'd forgotten it's Sunday—this is Visiting Day."

"And you robbed that man?" said Mrs. Pollifax incredulously. "He looks extremely difficult to take anything from. Should I know who he is?"

"Well, I don't want you fainting, my dear Mrs. P., but he's a sheik, a bona fide sheik."

"Ah," she said with pleasure, "they really do exist then! But no longer, I take it, on the desert?"

Robin grinned. "Not when they belong to one of the world's richest families, although I think he still spends a good bit of the year with his people. But not in a tent. Kashan's at least a generation away from all that, it was his grandfather who rode camels with the wind. Kashan's father discovered he was encamped on some of the world's richest oil fields in the Middle East, and Yazdan's the new breed. Went to Oxford, as a matter of fact, and then became a playboy and left jewels lying around carelessly—at least he was damned careless in Paris when I ran into him in '65."

"And now?"

"Now he's nearly forty and I hear he's a nut on religion and doesn't leave jewelry around. He reads the Koran instead."

"He's not reading it now," pointed out Mrs. Pollifax. "He's come to Montbrison to visit Mr. Sabry. What country is Mr. Kashan from?"

Robin gave her a quick glance. "Frankly I haven't the foggiest, I'm afraid all those deserts are one big blur to me." He sighed. "I suppose I should feel sentimental about the chap—he was my first really big job and it went off like peaches and cream and gave me no end of confidence."

"Which deserted you rather abruptly a minute ago," pointed out Mrs. Pollifax.

"Well, I told you it was my first major job; I had to remind myself for months afterward that he could afford the loss." He added indignantly, "I hope you don't think I became a criminal *easily.*"

"Not at all," she murmured, "but there must be some way to make an honest man of you."

Hafez walked slowly across the lawn toward them and when he reached them twined one arm around Mrs. Pollifax's chair and hung on it. "There's going to be Wiener Schnitzel for lunch," he confided. He addressed this information to Mrs. Pollifax but his gaze rested on the two men under the pink lawn umbrella.

"Do you know Mr. Sabry, the man in the wheelchair, Hafez?" she asked, watching his face.

"Yes, madame, he has the room across the hall from me."

"But did you know him before you came to the Clinic?"

He shook his head. "No, madame."

She hesitated and then she added, "And Mr. Kashan, the man visiting him, do you know him?"

Hafez's eyes blazed before he dropped his gaze to the ground. "I know him," he said tonelessly.

"Is he from Zabya then?"

"Yes, madame." He lifted expressionless eyes and added, "I will go to lunch now, I think. *Bon jour.*"

Robin watched him leave and then lifted an eyebrow at her. "I must say that was a strange bit of dialogue. You sounded rather like the Inquisition."

"And Hafez like a robot," she said thoughtfully, "which means, I think, that we just had a fairly important conversation."

Twelve

The sheik lunched with Ibrahim Sabry

in the dining room. Their heads remained close together at the table as they engaged in energetic conversation, frequently with gestures, but all of it too muted for Mrs. Pollifax to overhear. Court arrived a few minutes after Mrs. Pollifax, calling breathlessly across the tables, "I've been playing the organ again. Will you be in the garden this afternoon?"

Mrs. Pollifax nodded; she had no intention of being anywhere else. For the genuine convalescent there was the gift of shapeless time: naps, sunbath, small walks, massages, but she could scarcely call herself convalescent and time was working against her.

It was, therefore, in the garden that Court found her after lunch. "I want to talk to you," she said, striding toward her across the lawn. "I have to talk to you. Do you mind awfully?"

Mrs. Pollifax had been watching Sheik Kashan wheel

Sabry into the gazebo; the wheelchair was barely narrow enough to fit through the door so that for a moment the structure shuddered threateningly. It was not the sturdiest of gazebos, anyway, being fashioned entirely of bamboo. Now Sabry was safely within, and the Sheik had seated himself at the round table inside and was pulling papers from an attaché case.

She turned her attention to Court just as the girl slipped into a chair beside her. "I'm available," she told her, smiling.

Court looked close to tears. "I came back from the village this morning," she said, her voice trembling, "and I packed my suitcase and then after lunch I went up and unpacked it again."

"For myself I'm not that fond of packing," put in Mrs. Pollifax mildly, "but I daresay it's a form of exercise."

Court grudgingly laughed. "I'm sounding the idiot, of course." She pulled a handkerchief from her purse and blew her nose. "I thought perhaps if I talked to you—I simply don't know what to do, I ought to leave, I know it, but—"

Mrs. Pollifax said gently, "Perhaps if you'd tell me just what seems to be the matter—"

"Oh," said the girl angrily, "I don't want to fall in love again, that's what's the matter. And of all people with *him.*"

"Ah," said Mrs. Pollifax, enlightened at last. "We're talking about Robin. Are you about to fall in love with Robin?"

"Love," said the girl scornfully. "And he's so much like Eric." She shivered. "I can't bear that."

Mrs. Pollifax understood that there was going to be nothing rational about this conversation and adjusted herself to the fact. "Eric," she said pointedly.

Court's chin went up. "I *could* say that Eric abandoned me in every capital in Europe. As a matter of fact I *will* say it because it's what he did. I've been so careful," she

explained, "I've gone to such lengths to avoid entangle-
ments. I've dated only simpletons, frauds and ridiculous
creatures I couldn't possibly care about, and then I come
here and—" She turned to Mrs. Pollifax angrily. "Last
summer there wasn't anyone here under forty. Not a soul.
And this summer—I'm disintegrating," she wailed. "I'm
usually so poised, so calm, so—so—"

"Controlled?" suggested Mrs. Pollifax, handing her a
fresh handkerchief. "You haven't told me who Eric is, by
the way."

"My husband," said Court, blowing her nose again. "Or
was," she added, wiping her eyes. "I married him when I
was eighteen and we were divorced when I was twenty and
that's eight years ago. Mrs. Pollifax, I do want you to
know I had no intention of crying."

Mrs. Pollifax nodded. "One seldom does. So you were
married very young, and it wasn't a happy marriage, and
now Robin reminds you of Eric?"

She shivered. "The pattern's terrifyingly similar. Robin's so *attractive,* and there's all that charm and he doesn't
work for a living, which means no character at all. What
he does have is too much money and too much experience
—he's been everywhere, done everything, and known
everybody—and that's just how it was with Eric. They're
both playboys. I hate love," she announced, and after a
second's pause added ruefully, "It *hurts.*"

Mrs. Pollifax smiled. "I daresay you've gotten the worst
of it out of your system now and we can talk. But really
love has nothing to do with hurt, you know, it's we who
supply the wounds. Which—if I may risk offending you—
seems to be just what you're doing now."

"Given the circumstances, how?" demanded Court.

Mrs. Pollifax said dreamily, "I've often thought the
Buddhists are quite right, you know, when they say the
root of all suffering is desire. We're so full of greed, want-
ing this or that—to love or to escape love, to be this or be

that, to possess this or that. What do you think you'll accomplish by packing your suitcase and bolting?"

"I won't be hurt."

Mrs. Pollifax smiled. "I wonder if you can be sure of that. Of course you know very little about Robin but I wonder if you can be absolutely certain he's just like Eric. When you find out more about him there may be a few—well, surprises," she said, honestly enough. "For that matter you may not fall in love with him at all. Whatever makes you sure the future will be exactly like the past?"

"I don't know." Court shivered. "I don't know. But he—well, you see, he kissed me last evening in the library, while the film was being shown—"

"Ah," said Mrs. Pollifax, nodding.

"And—" She lifted her chin angrily. "And I thought—all right, I'll say it—I thought how wonderful it would be to marry and—and even have children. Which I can assure you was the furthest thing from my mind when I came here."

"Of course if you run away," pointed out Mrs. Pollifax, "you can't possibly have a baby."

"No," said Court miserably.

Mrs. Pollifax patted her affectionately on the arm. "What you need, I think, is a little bit of Zen."

"I beg your pardon?"

Mrs. Pollifax nodded. "Zen—tremendously refreshing. There's a great deal to be said for letting life just happen."

"Without *control?*"

"That's it, you see—without control."

"But—but that's *frightening!*" cried Court.

Mrs. Pollifax laughed. "On the contrary, it's much less painful than fighting every step of the way, and so much more delightful than trying to arrange life like a table setting, which one can never do, anyway. Really it's quite exciting to see what will happen along next," she added.

"At your age," said Court cautiously, "there are still surprises?"

Mrs. Pollifax beamed at her forgivingly. "Frequently, I can assure you, some pleasant and a few not at all pleasant, but of course one can't have the one without the other. It's impossible."

"Oh," said Court.

From the path behind them Robin called, "So there you are! I thought my two favorite ladies had vanished into thin air." He pulled up a chair and smiled at Court. "Where have you been all day?"

Mrs. Pollifax let Court reply while she glanced casually across the garden to the gazebo. The sheik had returned his papers to the attaché case and was standing as he talked to Sabry, delivering what looked to be an impassioned speech. Certainly Sabry was receiving it without his customary passiveness; his eyes gleamed and he looked almost exalted, yet even exaltation could not quite obscure the insensitivity of his face. How empty his eyes were, she thought idly; if he were not in a wheelchair, if he were not welded to it and helpless . . . if he were not confined . . . And suddenly the general's words yesterday slipped into her mind: *I have found this is not true of the professional killer who murders more than once, and in cold blood. It is a curious fact that it shows in the eyes, which I believe the poets call the windows of the soul. I have found the eyes of the habitual murderer to be completely empty. An interesting revenge by Nature, is it not?*

Sabry's eyes were empty, like stones.

Mrs. Pollifax suddenly sat upright in amazement, excited and a little breathless as she considered that wheelchair and the illusion it gave of immobility. If Sabry were not in that wheelchair . . . She thought in astonishment, "It's possible, it's terribly possible. He was even here when Fraser was here, Marcel said so. But how shocking that it's only just occurred to me." Doubt assailed her and she shook her head. "No, no, impossible—purest imagination," she told herself, but what a diabolically clever disguise it could be, she thought, and realized that even now she found it difficult, almost inhuman, to doubt a wheelchair.

Court and Robin were staring at her in surprise. "What on earth are you thinking?" demanded Robin. "You look as if you've just seen a ghost."

"Perhaps I have," she said, remembering the darkened hall last night, the sound of steps, and of heavy breathing in the stillness. "I was wondering what keeps Mr. Sabry in a wheelchair. What his particular illness might be."

Court looked taken aback but Robin's glance was thoughtful. "I see," he said softly. "Like Frankenstein you think he may—walk at night?"

"This is a day for wondering," she said.

"I heard it was multiple sclerosis," volunteered Court. "He came soon after I did, over two weeks ago. He takes whirlpool baths."

"Polio and strokes and broken limbs leave marks for doctors to see," mused Mrs. Pollifax, "but multiple sclerosis is a very slow disease, isn't it?" It made a good cover story. She was remembering Marcel's last words: *I will investigate thoroughly, I promise you,* and a picture came to her mind of Marcel entering Sabry's room, perhaps without knocking . . . Her eyes returned to the gazebo which was once again threatening to collapse as the sheik pushed Sabry's wheelchair through the arch. They moved to the shade of the poplar and a formal exchange of gestures took place, rather like two Frenchmen kissing and embracing. As he walked away the sheik turned and called over his shoulder, "I'll be back at six o'clock. Until then, *bkhatirrkoom.*" Smiling with the air of a man with many things to do, he walked quickly through the glass doors and vanished, leaving Sabry idle with a sheaf of papers in his lap. He began to sort and then to read them.

"What do you think?" asked Robin, watching her face.

"I think it's time I found out." She stood up. "Court, may I borrow Robin for a few minutes?"

"Of course," Court said, looking baffled.

Robin followed her across the grass to the ground-floor

entrance. Inside the door she turned to face him. "I want to get into Ibrahim Sabry's room and search it, Robin. Can you unlock his door for me?"

He glanced quickly out into the garden at Sabry. "That's a damned fool idea."

She tapped her foot impatiently. "There may not be another chance, Robin, it's a warm afternoon, it's nearing tea time and he looks settled under the tree. I want to find out if he's really an invalid. There has to be something, some hint—a pair of shoes with worn heels, a snapshot, even blood on his clothes if he was downstairs last night. Robin, do hurry!"

"All right," he said with a sigh. "Take the elevator, I'll meet you." He ran up the stairs two at a time and Mrs. Pollifax entered the elevator. At her floor she stepped out to wait, and after several minutes had ticked past Robin rejoined her. "I'm protesting this," he said angrily, "and I insist upon going in with you."

She said flatly, "Absolutely not. If anything happens— if he has hairy monsters waiting in his room to devour people—then you're the only one who knows what I've been up to."

His mouth tightened. "The balcony then. I'll stand on his balcony and not even breathe until you've left. For God's sake, woman, I can't chat amiably in the garden when I know you're in here. You're an amateur at this!"

She looked at him with exasperation but it was his skill that would unlock the door for her, after all. "All right," she said, "the balcony then," and led the way down the hall. Robin bent over the lock of number 153, the door opened and they entered Sabry's room.

"Now please—out of sight," she urged.

He moved across the room, stopping only to unlock the two doors of the huge wardrobe, which was fortuitous because they had not occurred to her at all. Blowing a kiss he slipped through the balcony door and was gone.

There was silence, and Mrs. Pollifax looked around her.

This room was darker than hers because it faced the mountain that hung over the Clinic but otherwise it was identical to her own. She hoped very much that it would yield something to support her suspicions. Going first to the desk she unearthed a number of papers, all of them written in Arabic. There were no snapshots. She turned to the right-hand side of the wardrobe that Robin had so thoughtfully unlocked for her and went through the five suits hanging there but she found no traces of blood on his clothes, nor were there any shoes in this side of the wardrobe. There was a suitcase, however, and Mrs. Pollifax removed it and carried it to the bed. It was a relatively small suitcase, 30″ in size and weighing roughly twenty pounds, she judged. An identification tag dangled from its handle and picking it up she saw to her surprise that it was not Sabry's suitcase. It belonged to the sheik, who must have brought it with him today. The tag read YAZDAN IBN KASHAN, and, underneath, a temporary address had been scribbled in pencil: *Suite I-A, Hotel Montreux-Palace, Montreux, Suisse*. That was where he was spending the night, then, and at six o'clock he would come back and pick up the suitcase. She leaned over the lock but it had been made doubly secure by the addition of two small brass padlocks, which she found curious. She half-turned toward the balcony and then reminded herself of Sabry. The suitcase could wait. Leaving it on the bed she returned to the closet to open and search the left side. She turned the knob, tugged and drew the door open.

Marcel's body, the upper half wrapped in glistening transparent plastic, occupied the entire half of the wardrobe, his spine curled into the foetal position, his head turned to one side, his vacant dead eyes staring straight into hers.

Mrs. Pollifax screamed.

She could not remember screaming before in her life. It was involuntary, an outraged protest, a reply to those staring, sightless eyes and to the shocked realization that his body had never been discovered at all. In the charged silence that followed her scream she heard the handle to the balcony door turn and then she heard the sound of running feet out in the hall and the door to the hall was thrown open. Sabry stood gaping at her. There was no sign of his wheelchair.

His glance moved from the suitcase on the bed to the opened door of the closet and his pale face turned scarlet. With three long strides he crossed the room, lifted his hand and struck her across the cheek. "Fool!" he gasped. "Idiot! Imbecile! Who are you?"

Mrs. Pollifax wordlessly shook her head.

He drew a gun from his pocket and tested its weight in one hand, his eyes malevolent, and then without another word he stalked out of the room across the hall and knocked with the gun at room 154. One of Madame Parviz's white-jacketed attendants answered the knock and Sabry gestured mutely at Mrs. Pollifax standing in his room. The man's eyes widened and he sucked in his breath with a hiss. Behind him Hafez appeared, and then the second attendant, both trying to look past Sabry.

Mrs. Pollifax had begun edging toward the hall when Hafez saw her. His mouth dropped open in astonishment. "Madame!" he cried in a shocked voice. "Oh, *madame!*" Darting under Sabry's arm he ran across the hall and flung his arms around her protectively.

"You know her!" accused Sabry, following.

"She is my friend Madame Pollifax," cried Hafez. "Don't you dare touch her, don't you dare!"

Sabry viciously slapped him. "You told her!"

The mark of the blow was livid on Hafez's cheek. "I did not," he gasped. "I did *not*. Monsieur, I beg of you. You think I risk Grandmama's life?"

Mrs. Pollifax stood listening and watching in fascinated horror. She made no move to speak or to act; a knot had just been untied and an unraveling had begun.

Sabry moved to the wardrobe and carefully locked both

doors again. "She has seen what is inside," he told them. "We must get her out of here."

"Injection?"

"No, no, too dangerous at this hour." He realized he was speaking in English and began to issue orders in Arabic. One attendant hurried down the hall and returned pushing Sabry's wheelchair, which he must have abandoned down the hall at the sound of her scream. To the second man, reverting to English, he said, "Get the car, Munir." To Munir's question in Arabic he said with a shake of his head, "No, no, we do nothing until we speak with Yazdan."

"What does he mean, the car?" whispered Mrs. Pollifax to Hafez.

His hand tightened convulsively in hers. "They are going to take you to the sheik, who left by car for Montreux fifteen minutes ago. They will ask him what to do about you. Madame, you are in great trouble."

"Yes," she agreed, nodding, but on the other hand she knew it was the price she had to pay for watching the pieces of the puzzle rearrange themselves.

Munir had vanished to get the car. She saw the second attendant emerge from Hafez's room wearing a sports jacket and slipping a gun into his pocket. Sabry sat down in the wheelchair and pointed to the suitcase lying on the bed. "Bring it to me, Fouad—place it on my lap with a blanket to cover it. Quickly! It's not to be left here again." To Mrs. Pollifax he said grimly, "You will be leaving the Clinic now for a pleasant little Sunday drive. The boy will go, too. You will walk quietly beside my wheelchair, looking as if you are pleased. If you make a move, if you call out, speak or try to signal anyone the boy will pay with his life, do you understand?" His eyes raked her face with a hatred that had all the impact of a blow.

"I understand," she said quietly. There was no need to speculate any longer about evil, she had just met with it, felt it, and it shook her.

"And you, Hafez," he continued softly, "you will recall your own situation and see that you behave. Serafina will remain with your grandmother. It needs only a telephone call—"

"I know," Hafez said in a strangled voice.

"Show them your gun, Fouad." He nodded as Fouad brought it from his pocket, displayed it and returned it to his pocket. "Good. We will go." His voice was contemptuous.

And so they began their exodus down the long, carpeted hall, a small, tightly knit group, a man in a wheelchair with a woman on one side, a boy on the other and an attendant behind; a kind of obscene Family Portrait for Visitors' Day, thought Mrs. Pollifax, and began to wonder what could be done. Nothing for the moment, she realized sadly. There was Robin. She was certain that he was safe but she had no idea how much he could have overheard from the balcony. Certainly he had heard her scream for she recalled the balcony door opening but it had quickly closed, which—under the circumstances—had saved him. Had he heard the footsteps running in the hall? If he had heard that much then he could have heard anything, and that was hopeful.

The elevator reached the Reception floor and the doors slid open. Sabry nodded to the head concierge behind the counter, they moved to the huge main door and Fouad neatly maneuvered the wheelchair down the steps. Just out of sight beyond the entrance Munir sat at the wheel of a long black limousine with the motor running. *I ought to scream,* thought Mrs. Pollifax, but she was paralyzed by the knowledge of how casually Sabry killed; he would think so little of a child's life or hers. Sabry issued more orders in Arabic and after a swift glance around him he climbed out of the wheelchair to take Munir's place at the wheel while Fouad folded up the chair and placed it in the trunk. The other attendant pushed Mrs. Pollifax and

Hafez into the rear, where Fouad joined them on a jump seat, his gun out of his pocket now and leveled at Hafez.

Slowly the car moved up the entrance drive past the greenhouse, entered the main road through the woods and headed toward the village. Mrs. Pollifax exchanged a glance with Hafez and tried to give him a reassuring smile that failed. She was wondering what Robin *could* do. She was realizing that the most obvious course, calling the police, would take an incredible amount of time and include complications and explanations beyond belief, and neither she nor Hafez had time. She began instead to think of what *she* could do, which was nothing for the moment, but when they reached Montreux, and the Hotel Montreux-Palace, she thought there might be possibilities if she kept her wits about her. She could not imagine another Family Scene moving through another lobby. Someone would be sent up to Suite I-A—Munir or Fouad, she presumed—to summon the sheik downstairs. That would reduce their captors by two, and no one in the group realized that she knew karate. If she and Hafez acted together they might overpower the remaining two men and escape. But not without the suitcase, thought Mrs. Pollifax; she was growing very interested in a suitcase with two extra locks that could not be left behind.

"Two quick karate chops to disable them," she said to herself. "Hafez open the car doors and I snatch the suitcase—" She fastened her gaze on the back of Sabry's neck and plotted the precise route of her karate strike while she tried not to think what would happen if she failed.

They reached Villeneuve and turned to the right along the waterfront, heading for Montreux. On their left Lake Geneva looked placid and washed of color in the late afternoon sun. Returning her glance to the back of Sabry's neck she inadvertently caught his eye in the rear-view mirror and hastily looked away, her glance falling to the mirror attached to the side of the car. In it, to her astonishment, she saw the reflection of a dark blue Mercedes convertible following behind them.

A dark blue Mercedes convertible . . .

Her heart began to beat faster. There was suddenly nowhere for her eyes to safely rest and she began to study the floor of the car and then the gun in Fouad's lap, snatching quick furtive glances into the mirror before dropping her eyes. It was impossible to see the driver of the Mercedes, or to read its license plate. She told herself there must be thousands of dark blue Mercedes cars in Switzerland, and dozens of them on this shore of the lake. On the other hand, this car was definitely dark blue and it was allowing other cars to pass while it remained at exactly the same distance behind them.

It was a wide road, with increasing traffic. Glancing past Sabry she saw a castle up ahead on the other side of the road, and for a moment her attention was pleasantly distracted by the sight of turrets, ancient stone walls and pointed clay tile roofs. She was staring at it when Fouad suddenly cried, *"Ha-sib! Ookuff!"*

Mrs. Pollifax turned her head and saw a flash of dark blue passing on their left. She caught a quick glimpse of a familiar profile—it was Robin—and saw his car surge ahead of the limousine. What followed happened all at once: the dark blue Mercedes cleared their car and slowed, Sabry leaned on his horn and cursed, the Mercedes braked and jerked to a stop and Sabry's car rammed it from behind with a crash and a grinding of metal.

Robin had just sacrificed the rear of his Mercedes convertible. For him, she thought, there could be no greater sacrifice.

Furiously Sabry tried to start up the limousine again but there were only ugly rattling noises. "Out!" he shouted. *"Ukhruj!"*

Doors opened and Mrs. Pollifax and Hafez were hustled outside to stand under the rock wall that rose almost perpendicular to that side of the road. Fouad's gun prodded her in the back. Mrs. Pollifax saw that the accident occupied most the the westbound lane to Montreux and that cars were coming to a standstill behind them. On the eastbound side the traffic moving toward Villeneuve was slowing to watch. The castle stood across the highway and an exodus had begun from the gates; several more hardy souls had already hurried to the center of the highway. Framed behind them stood a modest sign identifying the castle as the Castle de Chillon, open for tourists from 9 to 5.

Sabry cursed viciously. Turning to Fouad he snarled, "Get them out of here. Take them into the Castle—quickly, before a crowd gathers. Take this, too," he said, thrusting the suitcase at Fouad. "Come back in forty-five minutes. Hurry!"

For just a moment Mrs. Pollifax weighed the possibilities of running, but although Fouad's gun had been pocketed he held Hafez tightly by the arm. She and Hafez were thrust around the back of the car and out into the road where Robin and Sabry were confronting each other in fury. "You're damned right I cut you off!" she heard Robin shout. "How could I do anything else when you swerved out and accelerated at the same time? Somebody call the police!" he called across the road. *"Gendarmes! Polizei!"*

Good thinking, she thought.

Fouad hurried them across the highway, up the graveled walk and over a wooden bridge to the ticket booth where he shoved coins across the counter and held up three fingers. Just as the sound of a police siren rent the air they walked through the huge ancient gate and into an open, cobbled courtyard.

Thirteen

"*The rock on which Chillon stands,*"
said the guide, "was occupied by men of the Bronze Age and later by the Romans. The ancient road from Italy over Great St. Bernard was widened at the beginning of the eighteenth century. Chillon was built to guard the narrow defile between the lake and the mountains and to collect taxes on all merchandise that passed."

"I hope there are dungeons," said Hafez.

They stood in the courtyard at the edge of a tour group, and at Hafez's words Mrs. Pollifax turned to look at Fouad. Her impression was that he was angry and bored at the necessity of guarding a boy and an old woman. He gripped the suitcase with one hand while his right hand remained in his pocket curled around the butt of the gun but he looked cross and shifted frequently from one foot to the other.

"*Are* there dungeons?" Hafez asked Fouad.

With a martyred air Fouad handed each of them the printed map and leaflet that had been distributed at the gate without cost. She could sympathize with his predicament; he had hoped they might enter and sit somewhere for forty-five minutes, but it was Sunday, and the few benches in the courtyard were filled with people. There could be no entrusting Hafez to so intimate and lively a scene. It was necessary to keep them separated from the tourists and he had shrewdly guessed that the only way to accomplish this was to join the tourists. They were to remain just behind the tour group and speak to no one, he had told Hafez, and Hafez had obligingly translated his words to Mrs. Pollifax.

"There *are* dungeons," said Hafez, consulting the diagram, "but not yet. Not until we finish with the underground vaults." He lifted innocent eyes to Mrs. Pollifax. "Isn't it tremendous that there are dungeons?"

"Tremendous," she said gravely and wondered if he was receiving signals from her as clearly as she was receiving them from him. Yes but *wait,* she tried to tell with her eyes.

They passed under the windows of the caretaker's apartments and into the basement chamber of the castle, into a dim and medieval world of vaulted ceilings, ancient pillars and a floor of earth worn smooth by centuries. It was cool and dark in here; an arsenal, Hafez read aloud from his leaflet. The outside walls were striped with loopholes and through them Mrs. Pollifax could look out, almost at water level, and see Lake Geneva stretching flat and pale to the horizon, its waters gently lapping against the walls. "The dungeons are next," Hafez said, ignoring Fouad and speaking directly to her.

"Bonivard's Prison," said the guide in English after completing his first recitation in French.

"Dungeons," added Hafez triumphantly.

"This room dates from before the thirteenth century, when it was transformed and vaulted. It is here, in the fourteenth century, that Bonivard, Prior of St. Victor's in Geneva, remained chained to this fifth pillar for four years."

"Four years!" A murmur of incredulity swept through the group but Fouad took this moment to yawn. The pocket of his thin sports jacket sagged with the weight of the gun but his hand remained welded to it. The yawn was deceptive, she thought, stealing a quick glance at his face. He was stolid and gave every evidence of stupidity but he would be intelligent about his job, which was all that interested him. His dark eyes were alert and aware of every movement in the room. He knew she was watching him now and he turned and gave her a level, expressionless stare. She smiled vaguely and leaned nearer to hear the guide.

". . . because he was favorable to the Reformation, you see, which he wished to introduce to Geneva. He was freed in 1536 by the Bernese, and was immortalized by the English poet Byron, who has scrawled his name on this third pillar."

The group swerved toward the third pillar and Hafez started to go with them but Fouad reached out and pulled him back. *"La!"* he said flatly.

Certainly this was a grim place to spend four years, thought Mrs. Pollifax: a cold earthen floor, a low ceiling —he couldn't even have seen the water from the pillar to which he'd been chained. Recalling the equally grim circumstances that might await her and Hafez she glanced at her watch: it was 4:25 and they had been in the castle for twelve minutes. Fouad would return them to the highway at five o'clock—but that was the closing hour, she remembered soberly. She glanced at Hafez, who said quickly, "Next we go through the second courtyard and then into the Grand Hall of the High Bailiff."

He was offering her possibilities, she realized, but all of them were limited while they dogged the steps of the tour group. She knew what Hafez had not yet learned, that groups were unwieldy, slow to react to sudden jolts and frequently composed of people who did not appreciate having their peace disturbed. Fouad already knew this. There was no appeal that either of them could make to a group. As to separating themselves from it Hafez could outrun Fouad but Mrs. Pollifax could not. Fouad, for the moment, held all the cards: a gun and a crowd of tourists.

Hafez was looking disappointed in her. She, on the other hand, had begun to feel hopeful. A small miracle had occurred, their trip to a distasteful unknown had been interrupted and she saw no reason to be led back to Sabry like a lamb to the slaughter. No rational alternative presented itself but waiting did not bother her: it would give Fouad more time in which to grow bored. And so, having a gift for enjoying the moment, she gave herself over to medieval history and the enchantment of the castle. And it really was enchanting . . . They moved up a narrow wooden staircase to the next level and into the Grand Hall of the High Bailiff.

"Savoy period," Hafez read aloud. "In 1536 the Bernese divided the hall into three, their 'Grand Kirchen' being to the north. The separating walls were removed in 1836."

Again Fouad yawned.

They moved on, through the Coat-of-Arms Hall, the Duke's Chamber, several apartments and then a chapel, where they lingered before they filed through a passageway up into the Grand Hall of the Count. "Now called the Hall of Justice," recited Hafez, consulting the leaflet. "In the Middle Ages used for receptions and banquets. The tapestry hangings are all thirteenth century, the fireplace and ceiling are fifteenth century."

The hall was large, high-ceilinged and uncluttered but what impressed Mrs. Pollifax more than its history was its immediacy to the lake. Casement windows stood open to the sun and to the breeze from the water, and window seats had been built under each window so that she could imagine the lords and ladies of the castle contemplating the sun's rising and setting with a tranquil heedlessness of time. The windows were the real furnishings of the room, which was empty except for the ancient tapestries on the wall and huge carved, wooden chests placed here and there in corners.

Chests . . . Mrs. Pollifax felt a quickening of interest. Pausing beside one she ran her hand over its carving, noting the interstices in its serpentine design, and then casually placed one hand under the lid and discovered that it opened without resistance. It was empty except for a coil of thick rope, and she quickly closed it. Standing next to Fouad, Hafez had followed her investigation and he tactfully glanced away. Turning to Fouad he said, "It's like the old castle at home, is it not, Fouad? Look, madame, next comes the torture chamber and then what they call here a *Latrinehaus,* and then—" Fouad gave him a bored glance that silenced him.

It was now fifteen minutes to the hour. Lingering in the torture chamber, which Fouad seemed to regard with relish, she heard someone up ahead call out in English, "Latrines! Oh, do look!" Fouad pulled himself out of his reverie and signaled them to follow the group out of the torture chamber and into the high-ceilinged room adjoining it. The group pushed into one corner before it dispersed but when Fouad beckoned her on, Mrs. Pollifax firmly shook her head. "I want to look, too," she told him. "I've never felt that history books satisfactorily explained the hygienic arrangements of the past."

Reluctantly, with a martyred sigh, Fouad led her and Hafez to the corner and Mrs. Pollifax lifted a heavy wooden cover. She found herself looking straight down a cobblestoned, chimney-like chute, long since sanitized, to the shallow water of the lake below. "Why—how astonishing," she said. It was almost dizzying to look down from this height at water lapping against the rocks. "And how ingenious," she murmured.

She stood without moving, suddenly alert as she realized that the tour group had moved on to the next room— she could hear their voices grow fainter—leaving her and Hafez alone with Fouad. It was now or never, she reflected, and tentatively, hopefully, flattened her right hand, waiting.

"We go now," said Fouad, and moving up behind her he tapped her on the shoulder.

Mrs. Pollifax turned. With the velocity of a coiled

spring her hand struck Fouad in the stomach. He gasped, dropping the suitcase. As he doubled over clutching his middle she stepped back and delivered a karate chop to the base of his skull. He staggered to his knees, lingered a moment and then slowly fell to the floor unconscious.

"Mon Dieu!" gasped Hafez. "That was karate!"

"I don't think I killed him," Mrs. Pollifax said earnestly. "Quickly, Hafez, that chest in the corner over there, Hurry—before anyone comes."

He sprang into action with joy, propping open the chest and running back to help. "But he is big, he is heavy, madame!"

"He certainly is," she gasped as they dragged him across the stone floor. Lifting and pushing they succeeded in rolling him over the side until the rest of him fell in, too.

"Will he still breathe?" asked Hafez.

"If this chest is like the ones in the other room—yes, it is, see? There are holes among the carved decorations for ventilation."

"So there are. Don't forget his gun," pointed out Hafez, and retrieved it from Fouad's pocket and handed it to her. They closed the lid of the chest just as the next tour group entered the adjoining torture chamber, and, by the time they crossed the threshold of the room, Mrs. Pollifax and Hafez were sitting on the chest talking amiably, the suitcase between them.

"How long will he be—uh—indisposed, madame?" asked Hafez politely.

"I'm trying to remember. It's so difficult, a matter of pressure points and degrees, and of course no one gets hurt in class. I hit him in the right place but I don't know how hard," she explained, frowning over it, and then gave up. "Anyway, let's not wait and see, let's *go*."

They caught up with the original tour group and passed them at the entrance to the Defense Tower. Instead of joining them, however, they hurried down wooden stairs and across the open drawbridge to the steps leading into the courtyard. "We left Fouad in *Latrinehaus XIII*," Hafez said, squinting at the diagram.

"May he rest in peace," she added piously. "Here's the courtyard, Hafez, put away your literature and let's see if we can get out of here without being seen."

From behind a low wall they assessed the main courtyard and the entrance gate. The little souvenir house beside the gate was being locked for the night by a guard, and on the other side of the courtyard a second guard was closing the small dark entrance to the castle proper and drawing bars across the door. Closing time was two minutes away, realized Mrs. Pollifax with a glance at her watch. She took a step forward, looked beyond the gate and ducked back.

"What is it?"

"The other one, the thin one, Munir. He's just outside the gate watching everyone leave."

"But it's closing time!" cried Hafez. "What can we do? Where can we go?"

Mrs. Pollifax's eyes raked the courtyard but a castle that had stood guard against attack for centuries had not been built with a variety of entrances in mind, and according to the tour guide the few secret exits had long ago been sealed. There was only the one entrance through which to funnel the castle's pilgrims.

"If we can't go forward we'll have to go back," she said, and grasping his hand she hurried him across the courtyard and up the wooden stairs to the drawbridge. A guard called out to them. Mrs. Pollifax shouted back, "We've left our raincoats inside!"

"*Impermeables!*" called Hafez blithely, and they hurried across the drawbridge, passing both tour groups on their way.

"Closing time!" bawled the guide.

"*Impermeables!*" Hafez called back, giggling, and they plunged ahead through room after room until they reached the Grand Hall of the Count. When they stopped here to catch their breath the silence was sudden and disconcerting; a long shaft of late-afternoon sun reached the middle of the room and their haste had sent dust motes swirling up the golden beam. "The chests," Mrs. Pollifax said breathlessly. "This is the room with two chests. Climb inside, Hafez."

"I really don't want to but I will. What do we do after this?"

"For encores?" she said tartly. "We'll try again to get out when the castle's settled down." Crossing the room she lowered herself into the companion chest.

It was not a pleasant enclosure: it smelled of mildew and had the dimensions of a tomb. She was soon grateful for its protection, however, because some ten minutes later a guard entered the Grand Hall of the Count whistling cheerfully. He walked around the room, closed and locked the windows and went on to the next chamber. Mercifully there was no sound from Fouad in the room beyond, and soon both footsteps and whistling died away.

Half an hour later voices drifted up to them from the level below, and Mrs. Pollifax raised the top of her chest to listen. "But, monsieur, I cannot take you farther, as you can see the castle is empty and locked up for the night. I myself have inspected it. Nobody is here."

It was Sabry who replied but she could not hear his words. The guard's answer was impatient. "Monsieur, it is out of the question, it is against the rules. I cannot allow you upstairs, the castle is closed for the night." A door slammed, followed by silence.

The silence expanded and deepened, became drowsy with the somnolence of late afternoon's hush. Mrs. Pollifax closed her eyes, opened them and closed them again. The mildew seemed less potent, the warmth hypnotic. Over by the closed windows a trapped fly buzzed against the panes, endlessly, indefatigably . . .

Mrs. Pollifax awoke with a jolt and pushed open the

chest. It was still daylight; she saw by her watch that it was six-fifteen. *I mustn't do that again,* she thought, and climbed out of the chest to rouse Hafez. He looked up and waved a tiny flashlight at her as she lifted the top, and she saw that he'd been lying on his back playing tick-tack-toe on the lid of the chest with a piece of chalk. "What else do you carry in your pockets?" she asked with interest.

He stood up and from the pocket of his jacket drew out three marbles, a roll of tape, a jackknife, his tape recorder and a slice of Wiener Schnitzel in a soggy paper napkin. She smiled. "You might as well add Fouad's gun to your collection," she suggested. "I'll carry the suitcase. Let's take a look around now, shall we?"

He said doubtfully, "Do you really think they are convinced we're not here, madame?"

"No," she said, "but they might go away for a while. After all, if they had to consult the sheik once about us they may decide to do it again."

Hafez climbed out of the chest and pocketed the gun. Together they tiptoed through the cool, high-ceilinged rooms to the stairs by which they had gained the floor, but now they found the stairs concealed behind a closed door. Mrs. Pollifax rattled its latch but it did not budge. She ran her hands over the wood but it was a strong thick door with an ancient lock and no key. Hafez whispered, "It must have been locked from the other side, madame, or from this side with one of those old-fashioned big keys. Or perhaps it is barred?"

Mrs. Pollifax felt a sense of foreboding. This door, so huge and impregnable, was a surprise to her. She wondered how many other doors she had passed without noticing their existence. She and Hafez hurried back through the rooms toward the exit by which they had reentered the castle at five o'clock but here, too, their way was barred by a stout door, closed and locked. "Oh dear," said Mrs. Pollifax.

Hafez turned to look at her, his eyes huge. "We are locked in the castle, madame?"

"Yes," she said, and it seemed to her that her *yes* reverberated up and down the empty corridors and through all the empty rooms. Except the castle wasn't empty, she remembered. "Fouad!" she gasped.

They turned and ran back to the room where they had left him. Opening the chest Hafez said with relief, "He is still here, madame, may Allah be praised!"

He was still breathing, too, noted Mrs. Pollifax. He lay on his back, knees lifted, his eyelids fluttering as if he dreamed deeply. He gave no apparent signs of returning consciousness but she did not enjoy the thought of being locked in the castle with him. "There was rope in one of those rooms," she told Hafez. "We've got to bind his wrists and ankles or he'll spoil everything."

"I do not like him much," said Hafez, staring down at him. "If this was war I would shoot him, even if I am ten years old."

"Don't be bloodthirsty," she chided him. "Come, let's find the rope and tie him up—a gag might be in order, too —and then we'll have supper."

"Supper?"

"Well," she pointed out hopefully, "I was thinking of your Wiener Schnitzel, cut into equal portions with your jackknife. *If* you'd care to share it," she added politely.

Fourteen

In Langley, Virginia, it was mid-
afternoon. Carstairs inserted the key into the lock of his
office door and entered with a sigh of deep relief. He felt
he had been excessively well-behaved today. He had risen
at dawn, driven bumper-to-bumper to the golf club, await-
ed his turn in a milling crowd and played eighteen holes of
golf under a humid, 90-degree sun. His doctor had told
him the fresh air and exercise would rejuvenate him but
instead he felt hot, irritable, and betrayed. To a man accustomed to deploying live human beings around the
world he could think of nothing more idiotic than mind-
lessly pushing an inanimate ball around a green sward in
the sun.

Shrugging off his jacket he sat down at his desk and realized that with two hours of work he could clear away
last week's minutiae and begin the next seven days with a
minimum of encumbrances. His office was quiet and refreshingly cool. He could order coffee from the commis-
sary and later his dinner and in time he might forget his hysterical attempt to be normal. Normalcy, he decided without a flicker of regret, was simply not for him.

His buzzer sounded and he flicked on the switch. "Mr.
Carstairs, sir?" said the bright young voice from the covering office in Baltmore.

"Afternoon, Betsy," he said. "They've stuck you with
Sunday this week?"

"Yes, sir, and I was afraid you wouldn't be in the office this afternoon. I've a *most* peculiar call on the switchboard, sir. A Mr. Parviz insists on talking with you but he's not on our list at all. He's calling from Zabya."

"From *where?*"

"Zabya. Something about a cable you sent him. His English is either a little primitive or he's very upset, it's difficult to say which—and I might add that on top of that the connection's dreadful, too."

"He's certainly not one of ours," said Carstairs, frowning. "How the hell could he have gotten our unlisted number?"

"I've already asked him that, sir. Apparently he had the address, he turned it over to the Zabyan Embassy in Washington and they came through with the telephone number. Is the telephone company bribable, sir?"

"Not to my knowledge, and I can't imagine an embassy going to so much trouble, either. It'll be a damned nuisance if we have to change the number. Put the chap on my line so I can find out who the devil he is."

"Right, sir. A moment please."

Carstairs leaned over and switched on the tape-recording machine and sat back. There was a series of pops, followed by a peculiar underwater sound that occasionally accompanied transatlantic calls, and Carstairs heard a harsh, accented voice say, "Mustapha Parviz speaking. I am connected with Mr. William Carstairs, please?"

"You are, sir. What can I do for you?"

"I am calling in reference to the cable I received from you early today. You have just arrived back in America?"

"Just arrived back?" echoed Carstairs.

"Yes, I received your cable at noon here by Zabyan time. This is Mr. William Carstairs of the Legal Building in Baltimore Maryland, of the United States, who sent to me the cable from Europe?"

"Ah, the cable," said Carstairs craftily.

"Yes. It is most urgent, sir—I must learn the circumstances under which you saw them. Are they safe? Did you actually see them? Are they in Montreux?"

Castairs stiffened. "Montreux!" he exclaimed. "In Switzerland?"

The man at the other end of the line drew in his breath sharply. "You are playing with me, sir. I implore you —you must know this is of the gravest urgency, a matter of life and death. Where are they?"

Carstairs said swiftly, "I think we might clear this up very quickly, Mr. Parviz, if you'll just read me the cable."

The voice turned cold. "If you sent it, sir, I scarcely need read it to you."

"But you say that you received a cable from Montreux today, and in tracing it you discovered it was sent by—"

"You don't know." The voice broke. "You did not, then, after all—oh my God," the man said, and hung up.

Carstairs stared at the telephone in astonishment. After a moment he leaned over and switched on the recording machine and played the tape, listening carefully. Mustapha Parviz—the name struck him as vaguely familiar. *Where are they? Are they safe? Did you actually see them? . . .* Parviz had lost or misplaced something, documents or people, and it had something to do with Montreux. A matter of life and death . . . There was no mistaking the desperation in that voice; it had been studiously disciplined to the point of curtness but there were the revelatory small breaks, the quick intakes of breath, culminating in that bleak cry, *You don't know—oh my God.*

It was obvious that Parviz had no idea to whom he was speaking. It was equally obvious that he didn't care; he wanted only one thing, information, but without volunteering any in return. He'd been given the Baltimore address, but with neither explanation nor telephone number, and he'd desperately hoped—but how could he have gotten the address? Who would have sent him a cable bearing Carstairs's name?

He picked up the telephone and put through a call to Bishop on the off chance that he might be spared an hour's hunt through the files. Bishop wasn't at home but he was given a Georgetown number and presently he captured him on the phone.

"It's Sunday," Bishop reminded him. "Day of rest and gladness, remember? I'm at a party with a stunning blonde."

"Congratulations," Carstairs said dryly. "Now can you possibly tell me why the name of Mustapha Parviz sounds familiar to me?"

Bishop sighed. "Because he's in the Zabyan report we did for the State Department last week, file Z1020 if I'm not mistaken. Except it's not just Mustpaha Parviz, it's *General* Mustapha Parviz. He's head of the Zabyan army."

"Good God," said Carstairs.

"Don't you remember the Jonathan and David bit? Parviz, son of a poor tentmaker, brought to the palace to be schooled with Jarroud so that the future king would rub shoulders with the poor? Later there was a commission to military school and then he saved Jarroud's life in '60 by taking a bullet in his shoulder intended for Jarroud. Now Jarroud's the king and Mustapha's General of the whole shebang."

"A fact he neglected to mention," mused Carstairs. "One more question, Bishop. If someone—and I can assure you it wasn't I—sent a cable from Montreux giving the sender's address as William Carstairs, the Legal Building, Baltimore—"

Bishop interrupted. "That could be only one person, sir —Mrs. Pollifax."

"You're quite sure?"

"Oh yes, we've only two investigative agents in Switzerland this week and one of them has no knowledge at all of the Baltimore covering address. Interpol doesn't have it, either; they contact us directly."

Carstairs sighed. "I don't know why I resisted thinking of it but of course it's just the sort of thing she'd do."

"Is Mrs. Pollifax into something, sir?"

Carstairs said testily, "For heaven's sake, Bishop, she's been there only two days."

"Three days now, sir," pointed out Bishop with maddening precision, "It's already Sunday evening in Europe. Do you want me at the office?"

"No, but you might stay available while I contact Schoenbeck in Geneva. I'll call you back."

He hung up, consulted his file and asked that a call be put through to Schoenbeck's office. While he waited he used another phone to order a pot of coffee and then drew out file Z1020. He was studying it with concentration when his call to Geneva came through. "Schoenbeck?" he snapped.

But Schoenbeck was out. A cool, formal voice explained that this was his assistant speaking and that Schoenbeck had left Geneva several hours ago. Could his assistant be of help?

"The biggest help you can give me is to tell me how I can reach him immediately. This is Carstairs in Washington, about the Montbrison business."

"Ah yes, of course," said the assistant in well-modulated tones. "It is the Montbrison case, monsieur, that has taken him from Geneva today. He left in midafternoon to confer with M. Gervard. Unfortunately he is not returned yet."

"What time is it over there?"

"Nine o'clock, sir, in the evening."

"And he's not back yet?"

"No, monsieur."

Carstairs said abruptly, "Something's happened then? Look here, we've an agent at Montbrison, too, and I've had a most peculiar telephone call—"

The voice was soothing. "No, no, monsieur, it had nothing to do with your agent Mrs. Pollifax. It is our agent who has disappeared for the moment. We are making inquiries."

"Disappeared!" exclaimed Carstairs. "Marcel?"

"It will be cleared up, I am sure," the voice went on with the blandness of a doctor reassuring a terminal patient. "It is M. Schoenbeck's urgent hope that cover need not be broken and so he consented to help with inquiries, very discreetly."

"When did you last hear from Marcel?" demanded Carstairs. "And what was on his mind?"

"His last report was yesterday—Saturday—at the usual hour of five o'clock, monsieur. As to what was on his mind—" The voice hesitated and then turned silky. "He mainly expressed some doubts about your agent, sir."

Carstairs's voice became even silkier. "May I ask why?"

"But of course, monsieur. He had requested her to make the acquaintance of a man named Burke-Jones, about whom serious suspicions have been aroused, and she did this. But she became quickly distracted by a small child staying at the Clinic. Marcel had begun to feel the maternal instincts had blunted her—uh—shall we say perceptions?"

Carstairs said curtly, "You may tell Schoenbeck that Mrs. Pollifax is distracted by everything that comes her way but never to the detriment of the job. Her distractions are notorious but never without point. When was Marcel's next contact to be made?"

"He should have telephoned this morning, monsieur, before going to work at the Clinic."

"But that's nearly fifteen hours ago!"

"Yes, monsieur. Naturally we have made discreet inquiries. He did not return to his room in the village last night."

"Has my agent been told about this?"

The voice was polite "A call was attempted, sir. I put it through myself, after working out the code for it and asking her to make inquiries about Cousin Matthew. Unfortunately your agent had just left for a little drive with friends."

"What friends?"

The voice was disapproving. "I'm sure I cannot tell you, sir, but Monsieur Schoenbeck will contact you upon his return."

"Do that," said Carstairs. "I'll wait for his call." He hung up and swore steadily. He was still swearing when Bishop telephoned, and when he had finished, Bishop said mildly, "You're upset."

"You're damned right I'm upset. I've been talking with a Pollyanna in Schoenbeck's office who informs me that Marcel hasn't reported in for fourteen and a half hours but everything's all right."

"It doesn't sound all right to me," said Bishop.

"Bless you for that," breathed Carstairs. "Well, there's nothing to be done for the moment except wait for Schoenbeck's call. You can return to your day of rest and gladness, Bishop."

"Thank you, sir. Are you worried?"

"I don't know," fretted Carstairs. "It's maddening not to be in charge myself, and still more maddening to think how easily they could blow this. Schoenbeck is so damned cautious, so damned discreet. It inhibits him."

"Well, sir, my blonde is gorgeous but not quite so diverting as Mrs. Pollifax. Give me a ring if something comes up."

"Yes," said Carstairs and hung up with a sigh, knowing that if one of his agents had been out of contact for nearly fifteen hours in a closed situation like this he certainly wouldn't be driving off to a rendezvous to discuss it, he'd be tearing the Clinic apart and to hell with everybody's cover stories. "Too damned polite," he growled and began to consider a few things he could do from this end that, hopefully, wouldn't irk Schoenbeck. He could, for one thing, telephone Mrs. Pollifax and make certain that she was all right, and he could discover just why she had sent a cablegram in his name. Schoenbeck wouldn't care for his meddling but Mrs. Pollifax was *his* agent, after all.

He put through a call to the Hotel-Clinic Montbrison and it was placed before he had finished his cup of coffee. Whoever was on night duty over there spoke a disjointed English, and guessing the man's accent Carstairs switched to Italian. Even in Italian, however, he couldn't reach Mrs. Pollifax because there was no answer to the telephone in her room. This was worrisome because if it was nearly ten o'clock in the evening over there she ought to be getting ready to signal from her balcony. He asked a few questions about schedules at the concierge's desk and the porter replied, adding a few complaints as well.

"Who was on duty this afternoon?" Carstairs asked. He nodded and wrote down the name and home telephone number of the head concierge, thanked the porter and hung up.

Consulting the code given Mrs. Pollifax he picked up the telephone and asked that a cable be sent to her at Montbrison. "Take this down," he said and dictated: "URGENTLY REQUEST EXPLANATION CABLE SENT IN MY NAME SUNDAY STOP UNCLE BILL ON THE LOOSE AGAIN IN FRANCE STOP WHERE IS COUSIN MATTHEW STOP ARE YOU RUNNING A TEMPERATURE STOP LOVE ADELAIDE. Got that?"

"Yes, sir."

"Now get me Switzerland again." He frowned over the name of the head concierge. "A Monsieur Piers Grundig, in St. Gingolph." He began to feel the satisfaction of working through some of his frustrations and was just congratulating himself about it when Bishop walked in. "What on earth!" he said in surprise.

"Couldn't help it, sir," said Bishop cheerfully. "Something's up, isn't it? It was beginning to interfere with both the rest and the gladness. What do you *think* is up?"

Carstairs shrugged helplessly. "I wish I knew. Marcel disappeared from view sometime between five o'clock Saturday and seven o'clock this morning their time, and in

midafternoon today Mrs. Pollifax went for a drive—with
friends, I'm told—and she doesn't seem to have returned
yet. Marcel's missing and I'm beginning to think Mrs. Pollifax is missing, too. And I had that damned mysterious
call from Parviz. Hello?" he barked into the phone. "Is
this Piers Grundig, head concierge at the Hotel-Clinic
Montbrison?" He waved Bishop to sit down.

His questions to the man were concise and organized.
He had seen Madame Pollifax leave? She had gone for a
drive with people from the Clinic? She had left at what
hour? And the names of the friends, he inquired as he
reached for pencil and paper.

"Monsieur Sabry, yes," he said, writing busily. "Two
gentlemen not familiar to you, and the boy Hafez. Hafez
what?" He looked astonished. "Parviz," he echoed in a
hollow voice. "Yes, I see. Thank you very much, Monsieur Grundig, I'm obliged to you."

He hung up, and seeing his face Bishop said, "Trouble."

"Trouble or a very remarkable coincidence," growled
Carstairs. "I don't like it."

"Your intuition's usually right, And no Schoenbeck
yet?"

"No Schoenbeck yet." Carstairs looked grim. "I gave
Mrs. Pollifax to Interpol like a gift and they give every evidence of having discarded her like a boring Christmas
tie."

Bishop said soberly, "Well, you know she doesn't look
like a gift at first glance, sir. She confuses people by looking the nice cozy grandmother type."

"This time she seems to have confused the wrong people," Carstairs said harshly. "She's confused Interpol but
I'm beginning to have the acute feeling that *someone* has
seen through the façade and discovered she's dangerous.
And Interpol is the last to guess this." He lifted his glance
to Bishop. "There's a damned busy week ahead, Bishop,

but it's time someone translates Mrs. Pollifax to Interpol. Is your passport available?"

Bishop brightened. "In my desk, sir."

Carstairs nodded. "I'll call a taxi for you. I want you to take along the tape recording of Parviz's call, and I want you to give it to Schoenbeck, but first—I repeat *first*—you're to find out where the hell Mrs. Pollifax is." He glanced at his watch "It's half-past four, Bishop, you've just time to catch the six o'clock plane to Geneva. It will get you to Geneva—given the time differences—by seven-thirty tomorrow morning."

"On my way, sir," said Bishop, snatching up the tape and his jacket.

"Oh and Bishop—"

He turned at the door. "Yes, sir?"

"For God's sake keep me posted."

"Yes, sir," he said, and the door slammed behind him.

Fifteen

It was nearing midnight and it seemed to Mrs. Pollifax that it had been dark forever. In fact it had grown dark inside the castle long before the last rays of sun fled the lake and the sky outside. Around eight o'clock they had divided Hafez's small hoard of Wiener Schnitzel but that, too, felt a long time ago. After a sojourn in each of the rooms they had settled in the Hall of the Count, where Mrs. Pollifax sat on the floor, her back against the wooden chest. Odd little noises punctuated the silence: the scurrying of mice, the explosive creak of wood as the temperature dropped, the sound of waves from a far-off boat lapping against the outer walls. From time to time she lighted a match from the package that Bishop had given her in New York and when she did this, to glance at her watch, the flare of light would pick out the suitcase beside her and the small arsenal in her lap: Hafez's jackknife, Fouad's gun and a segment of the rope that wound up to the pile she had placed on the chest. At the moment Mrs. Pollifax would gladly have traded them all for a warm coat and some food. "What are you doing now?" she called softly to Hafez.

"I am at the window, madame, looking at the stars. I can see the head of Ursa Major, the Great Bear, and also the Chair of Cassiopeia. Oh, I wish you could see the stars in the Rub' al Khali, madame, they shine so clear, so bright." He came back to sit down again beside her.

"The Rub' al Khali?"

"It's called also the Empty Quarter—except it is not empty, you know. Sometimes—sometimes my father has taken me there, and we camp out at night under the stars and they come near enough to touch. There are desert gazelles there, too. I shall be an astronomer when I grow up," he said firmly.

"Then we must make certain that you grow up," she said lightly. "Go on with your story, Hafez, I want to know everything."

"Yes," he said with a sigh, "but it is all so unpleasant and the stars so beautiful. Where was I? Oh yes, after finding me in the bazaar Munir drove me to the Zabyan airport but my father was not there at all, as you can guess. Fouad kept saying, 'He is inside the plane, they're giving him oxygen until the doctor comes.' So I ran across the runway to the plane and up the steps but my father was not there at all. Instead Grandmama lay stretched out on three seats, quite unconscious."

"Drugged," nodded Mrs. Pollifax.

"Yes. And as I went to her they closed the door to the plane and that's when I understood they had tricked me and nothing at all had happened to my father. The plane took off two minutes later."

"How many of them were there?"

"There were two pilots but I did not see them again. There was Serafina, who seems to be a nurse. There was Fouad and Munir, and a man I think was a steward and belonged to the plane because he wore a uniform and served food to me. We had one meal and I think it was drugged because I fell asleep afterward. When we landed I could scarcely believe we had flown all the way to Switzerland. That was when Mr. Sabry came on board to—to—" He sighed. "To explain."

"That you were hostages," said Mrs. Pollifax, nodding.

"Yes, madame. He said we were going to a very nice place, a Clinic, and I would be free to walk around and enjoy myself but my grandmother would be kept prisoner in her room. If I breathed a word of it, if I begged help or confided in anyone my grandmother would be given an injection that would kill her at once. He said Fouad and Munir would always be with her and that whether she lived or died would be up to me."

" 'An intolerable tension,' " remembered Mrs. Pollifax aloud, and her shiver was not from the cold. She could believe their threat; they really would dispose of Madame Parviz—and still could—with a quick and ruthless indifference. "And so your grandmother has been kept drugged ever since you came."

"Yes, madame."

Mrs. Pollifax smiled faintly. "Until you stole thirteen aspirin from me, Hafez?"

"You saw that, madame?" He turned and looked up at her, his face a pale oval in the darkness.

"I saw. I guessed that after the initial injections they must be giving your grandmother pills that looked just like aspirin. You planned a little sleight of hand."

"It was all I could think to do," he said, his voice trembling a little. "There were thirteen pills in the bottle next to Grandmama's bed. I replaced them with thirteen aspirin. I thought if Grandmama could once wake up we could talk of what to do. And she did wake up," he added proudly, "She said we must be very brave and cable my father that we are safe—even if we are not safe—and then place our lives in the hands of Allah. But, madame—" She saw the flash of his smile. "She did not know that you would help, too. Do you think Allah sent you?"

"The CIA sent me," she said dryly, "and I've never heard them accused of god-like qualities."

"But she is unprotected now," he went on in a troubled voice. "Madame, I am very worried about her."

She groped for his hand and squeezed it. "I think she'll be all right while they look for you, Hafez. They're not desperate yet and two hostages are better than one. But what's behind all this, Hafez, have they told you?"

He sighed. "No, but I am sure it has something to do with my father being general of the Zabyan army."

"You mean *the* general?" Her knowledge of army hierarchies had never been clear and it had always seemed to her that generals tended to multiply like corporative vice-presidents or rabbits.

"Yes, madame. It's always been said that no one could ever use the army to overthrow the government as long as my father is general. Because he is very loyal, very dedicated to Jarroud's cause."

"They have found a way to divide his loyalties now," she pointed out softly. "I wonder what they're up to." A coup, probably, she thought. One began by blackmailing a general, who would then turn over his army or not turn it over, depending upon how vulnerable he was—but Parviz was vulnerable now, indeed. It was true that he could compromise by agreeing to keep his army out of the arena, but that would be just as effective for the coup-makers as joining them. In any direction he turned he would be rendered helpless. He could save his family or his king but it was unlikely that he could do both. It was a diabolical trap. It was also very well-planned, she realized, because Parviz would have had a week to search for his family and that was long enough to scour the Middle East but who would think of looking for them in a quiet convalescent clinic in Switzerland?

But although Mrs. Pollifax worked hard at picturing a coup d'etat in Zabya it remained an abstract for her, a geometry problem lacking flesh and bones. She had no passion for making or unmaking history. Rulers came to power and rulers lost their power through votes, old age or violence. They had their brief fling at immortality and departed; it was history's victims for whom she felt compassion. What mattered the more to her at this moment was keeping Hafez and Madame Parviz alive while the actors played out their intrigues on a stage elsewhere.

"This isn't a fair question, Hafez," she said, "but when

your father receives the cable sent this morning what do
you think he will do? What manner of man is he?"

"Well, he is a man of much integrity, madame. I cannot
imagine his turning over the country or the king to wicked
people." He sighed. "I do not know what he will do, madame. If he thinks me safe, and if they promise not to kill
the king—why, then, to save bloodshed he *might* do as
these people ask. But only to avoid a great bloodletting. I
don't know, you see."

If they would promise—she tried to think of what
promises a man like Sabry would keep. "What influence
has your mother?"

"Oh, she is dead, madame. When I was a child she
died."

"You're the whole family then?" She was startled.
"You, your grandmother, and your father?"

"Yes, madame."

Mrs. Pollifax shivered, and her list of victims expanded.
Even King Solomon, she thought, might have a little trouble with this one.

"My father loves the king, they are like brothers," went
on Hafez in a low voice. "My father says Jarroud thinks of
the people and wants them to be less poor, which really
they should be because the oil belongs to them. My father
was very poor once, too, madame. They say it is my father
who always reminds the king of the people." He hesitated.
"Madame, I cannot answer your question."

She nodded. "Of course you can't. Tell me instead
about the sheik. He's involved in this somewhere?"

"Oh yes, madame. It was his private plane that brought
us here to Switzerland. His plane has been pointed out to
me many times so I know this."

So there it was, thought Mrs. Pollifax, as the remaining
pieces of the puzzle slipped into place. She was remembering the king's birthday party on Tuesday—oh, perfect, she
reflected. The army would be much in evidence, out in
force and proudly displayed, yet every attention would be

diverted to the festival and to the visiting heads of state. Given the right coincidences, careful planning and shrewd arrangements the day would end with the king deposed or dead and the government taken over by—

By the sheik, of course, she thought. Of *course* the sheik. She remembered the flash of his smile, the dark handsome face of the man whom Robin had called one of the richest men in the world. She thought, *What does one do with so much money? He's already explored the world of the senses—of women, cars, jewels—and now he's moved on to the world of the ascetic, and he is still young. What next?*

She knew the answer because it followed a logical pattern: he would want power. Given power, he would be able to manipulate, to create and to change. It was the ultimate toy, the deepest psychological lust of all because it held within it all the satisfactions of the sensual as well as the ascetic.

Her hand moved to the sheik's suitcase behind her that had been so important to Sabry that it couldn't be left behind. I have Hafez and I have this, she thought, and wondered what they would do to get them back.

In the adjoining room Fouad moaned, and Mrs. Pollifax put away her thoughts and nudged Hafez. "We'd better look at Fouad," she told him, and distributing the contents of her lap she led the way into the next chamber. They bent over the chest with a lighted match. This time Fouad's eyes lifted to stare without intelligence at the pinpoint of flame above him. Another half hour or so, she guessed, and he would remember who they were and why he was in the chest.

She groped for a place to sit. "I have Hafez and I have their suitcase," she repeated . . . It must be one o'clock by now, already Monday morning. The caretaker of the castle would be asleep in his apartment by the gate, and the highway would be nearly empty of cars but she did not believe for a moment that Sabry had abandoned his post outside. At first he would have been angry, and then he would have been puzzled because Fouad was strong, shrewd, and armed with a gun. It would be inconceivable to him that Fouad could disappear in the company of an elderly woman and a boy. But that incredulity would have returned to anger by now, and given time to check and double-check she thought that Sabry must be quite certain the three of them were still in the castle. *Someone* would be on guard outside—waiting, watching . . .

Hafez tapped her on the arm. "What is it, madame, you sigh so heavily! And don't you prefer a chest? You are seated on the latrine."

"Latrine?" She was startled, and one hand moved to the ancient, splintery surface to discover that he was right, she was sitting on the long bench-top that concealed the latrine, while below—"Hafez!" she said in a surprised voice and began to smile in the darkness. "Hafez, I've been waiting for inspiration and you've just given it to me. *Think,* Hafez! Think what's below me!"

"Lake Geneva," he said doubtfully. "And rocks."

"No, no, a way out of the castle, Hafez. A way *out*."

"Down that chimney?" he said incredulously. "But, madame—how could one get down? It is two floors high, surely?"

"I'm thinking of the coil of rope," she told him eagerly. "I managed a rope once, over Robin's balcony. It will all depend on the strength of the rope. We must be resourceful, Hafez."

"Rope . . ." Hafez said reflectively, and his voice suddenly quickened. "Oh, *yes,* madame! Here, try it, feel it. Do you think—?"

"Let's tie it to the suitcase and drop the suitcase down the chute and see what happens," she urged. "Give me a hand, Hafez. Light a match."

Matches flared briefly, one after the other. They secured one end of the rope to the iron bolt of the window shutter on the wall nearby, and the other end she knotted to the handle of the suitcase. Gently they lowered the weight down the cute; it bumped softly here and there against the stones, and hung suspended, swaying back and forth.

"It didn't break," whispered Hafez. "How far down do you think it went?"

"I don't know," she said. "Twenty feet, thirty. It's a long rope." She was assessing twenty pounds of suitcase against Hafez's weight and her own and she was not sure that she liked the odds. To entrust their lives to a rope that had lain in a damp chest for days, months, even perhaps for years—

Hafez abruptly placed his hand on her arm. He said in a low voice, "Madame."

She heard it, too, and stiffened. Not far away—it came from one of the rooms nearby—a voice had lifted in momentary anger.

"Munir's voice," whispered Hafez. "Madame, they're *inside the castle.*"

Inside the castle . . . Her astonishment fought against the chill of terror. How *could* they be inside, what entrance had they discovered that she and Hafez had missed? She tried to think. A ladder? The thought of a ladder jarred her out of paralysis. If they had a ladder they could scale the outside wall and gain the lower roofs, and from there—yes, they could do it if the ladder was long enough—they could reach one of those barless windows on the stairs to the Defense Tower and this would bring them into the corridor two rooms away. There was no magic about it, then; they had brought equipment and were coming in after them.

She turned quickly to Hafez, her decision made for her, and placed the end of the rope in Hafez's hand. "Go first," she told him sternly, "hand over hand, not too fast. If I can't make it, take the suitcase to Robin. The walls will be near enough to touch with your feet if you panic."

"I do not panic," Hafez whispered scornfully, and she saw his shadowy form step over the side and vanish. The rope groaned a little, and behind her the shutter creaked as it felt his weight but the knots held, the rope remained steady.

In the chest across the room Fouad groaned and moved, one knee hitting the top of the chest with a thud. In the corridor beyond the chest a beam of light flashed across the stones, lifted and vanished. A low voice said, "Fool! Keep the light away from the window!" It was Sabry's voice. She climbed over the side of the opening and waited, holding her breath. When she felt two tugs on the rope she thought—madness!—but she didn't hesitate.

It was dark and cold in the chute. The rope strained at her weight. She placed a hand under her to check her descent but even so she went down in an insane rush. The weight of the suitcase had turned the rope into a plumb line so that it moved in slow giddy circles between top and bottom. Her hands burned from the coarse hemp. Down —down—Something brushed past her, wings fluttering, and then she reached the suitcase and dangled there uncertainly. "Jump, madame," whispered Hafez excitedly. "You've made it! It's not far."

She let go, slid across wet rocks and promptly sat down in the water, head spinning dizzily. "Please, madame—do hurry," gasped Hafez, cutting away the suitcase with his knife. "Quickly, madame!"

She stumbled to her feet. Hafez handed her the gun and the knife, lifted the suitcase and waded out of the opening into the shallows of Lake Geneva. She followed. The water was up to her knees. She had neglected to remove her shoes and the rocks underfoot were slippery with lichen. As they moved slowly around the castle in the direction of the shore she alternately stumbled, rose, slipped and fell again. She was drenched when they reached the cobbled shore and as she waded out of the water she stopped and looked up at the dark castle serrating the skyline. Suddenly a thin beam of light impaled her and vanished. Out of the darkness a familiar voice said, "Good God, it's really you?"

It was a voice from another world. Mrs. Pollifax stood uncertainly at the water's edge, caught in the act of wringing water from her skirts. "Robin?" she faltered.

"Over here—in a rowboat," came his stage whisper, and she heard the creak of oar locks and a muted splash of water. "Climb in," she heard him say, and then he added flippantly, "Whatever kept you so long?"

Sixteen

"*And now let's get the hell out of here,*"

Robin said, steadying her as she fell into the boat. "They've good ears, those two, they're at the gate." He sat down, picked up the oars and began to row.

"Monsieur, they are not at the gate," whispered Hafez, "they're inside the castle."

"Good Lord," he said, and rowed faster.

The darkness was thinning and shapes were beginning to separate themselves from the opaque blackness of night. She could see the point of land toward which Robin rowed, and then the silhouette of rocks through which he threaded the boat as he headed toward a more distant cove. He spoke only once. "Are those *teeth* I hear chattering?"

Hafez giggled.

"Yes," said Mrs. Pollifax with dignity. They rounded the point and a minute later the boat hit the graveled shore and ground to a stop. The castle could no longer be seen; it was hidden by trees.

"I've got a car," Robin said. "A rented one. It's up there off the road, straight ahead through the trees."

"You're a miracle, Robin," she said. "It's the greatest piece of luck your being here."

"Luck!" he growled, helping Hafez out with the suitcase. "It was getting too damned crowded at the front of the castle, that's all. The lake was the only place left for me. Could you hurry a little? The sooner we get out of this place the happier I'll feel. There's a blanket in the back seat of the car," he added. "Get moving while I tie up the boat."

When he joined them in the car Mrs. Pollifax and Hafez had already found the blanket and were huddled under it together. Climbing in behind the wheel he turned and gave her a stern glance. "Look here, I've never felt so helpless in my life," he said. "I've spent the whole night debating whether to go to the police, telling myself I'd call them within the hour, then postponing because I didn't want to upset your applecart, but don't you think it's time I drive like hell now to a police station?"

"Now?" gasped Hafez, and turning to Mrs. Pollifax he said desperately, "Madame, my grandmother—"

Mrs. Pollifax nodded. "Hafez is right, we *must* get back to the Clinic, Robin, it's where Sabry will head as soon as he discovers Fouad and learns how we've gotten away. There isn't time to go to the police."

Robin said incredulously, "We can be there inside of ten minutes."

"Yes and spend the next fifteen explaining to them. Robin, we must hurry to Madame Parviz—please!"

He angrily started the car. "Then you'd better explain to me what you found at the Clinic that's so important you go back. What *did* happen in Sabry's room?"

"Everything, and all of it ominous," she said grimly. "Hafez and his grandmother are hostages—"

"Hostages?"

"Yes, and Sabry's a murderer, and your old friend the sheik is heavily involved—"

"Yazdan!"

"And Serafina is guarding Madame Parviz, who's been kept drugged, and just one telephone call from Sabry could end her life and—"

"But this is incredible," protested Robin.

"Yes, isn't it? And Marcel—" Her voice broke. "Marcel's body is in Sabry's closet. That's why I screamed."

"Good God," he groaned. "You mean nobody knows he's dead except us?"

"Yes," she said, and sitting up saw that her words had at least effected a change in their speed for they were already entering Villeneuve. "We left Fouad tied up in a chest inside the castle but he was already beginning to stir and groan, and once they find him they need only telephone the Clinic, you see."

"I'm not sure they'll reach anyone—that night porter sleeps most of the night," Robin said dryly.

"Let's hope he's sleeping now!"

"But what are these demented people up to?" protested Robin as he guided the car at top speed through narrow streets and headed toward the mountains.

"I think a coup d'etat in Zabya," said Mrs. Pollifax. "The king is celebrating his fortieth birthday on Tuesday."

"But that's tomorrow."

"My goodness, yes," she said, glancing at her watch. "But what time is it?" she faltered, staring at a watch that said half-past midnight.

"Nearly four o'clock."

"Good heavens!" She held the watch to her ear and shook it. "My watch has stopped, I've lost three hours!"

"Be grateful, they were damned tedious hours, believe me."

She conceded this and sat back. It was no wonder, then, that Sabry and Munir had risked going into the castle after

them. They were obviously running out of time if they
planned to return to the Middle East today or tonight to
await a triumphant entry into Zabya tomorrow. If they
were leaving the Clinic so soon perhaps they had planned
to bury Marcel somewhere on the mountainside before
they left. She had certainly been naive about Marcel's
death: of course they couldn't risk the discovery of a
murder so soon after Fraser's questionable death. She had
assumed that employees of the Clinic had concealed the
tragedy when instead it was Sabry who had returned to the
Unterwasser Massage room, carried the body up to his
room and gone back to scrub away the blood.

And so neither the police nor Interpol knew that Marcel
was dead, and there was nothing to warn them of anything
wrong except that she had not signaled last night from her
balcony. She wondered what they were doing about that.
She tried to think what she would do if she were Interpol
but she was too tired, and anyway she had begun to suspect that Interpol did not expect a great deal of her. It was
Marcel who had direct lines of communication with them,
and from her they apparently wanted only reassurances
that she was all right. This was gallant of them if one enjoyed playing Boy Scout games with a flashlight at night
but it was of no particular usefulness when, as the expression went, all hell broke loose. Possibly a touch of male
chauvinism there, she thought; Swiss women had only just
won the vote, after all.

"Really," she said aloud in an exasperated voice, "nothing seems to be going as they expected. I think Interpol
has taken far too many precautions to keep everything un-
dercover. There's also this suitcase," she added, looking at
it speculatively.

"What suitcase?"

"You'll see it presently," she told him. "It has two padlocks on it beside the regular lock and I'm hoping you'll
open it for me, Robin. It belongs to the sheik, at least it

has his luggage tag on it, and Mr. Sabry seems to regard it as terribly important. Obviously it has something to do with the coup d'etat or whatever they're planning."

"I can hardly wait," Robin said lightly.

They had entered the village on the mountain, and turning the corner at high speed they surprised an old man sweeping the sidewalk with a broom. He jumped back from the curb, shaking his fist in indignation, and then they turned and drove down the narrow road along the ravine to the Clinic. It was still night here but the rising sun was dusting the mountain peaks with gold. The lake below was wrapped in a mist that drifted lazily with each stirring breeze.

Hafez said in an anguished voice, "We're almost there, but how shall we ever get inside the Clinic?"

"That you can safely leave to Robin," she told him wryly.

"But Serafina mustn't hear," he protested. "She'll be waiting for Mr. Sabry, and if she sees us without him—" His voice trembled. "You understand, monsieur, they kill so easily."

"That," said Robin grimly, "I'm beginning to understand." He turned off the engine of the car and coasted it down the incline past the greenhouse. Abreast of the main door it came to a halt. "Don't slam the car doors," he whispered. "Watch the gravel—stick with the flower beds. Tiptoe around the Clinic to the garden door."

A few minutes later they stood inside the Clinic on the ground floor next to the Unterwasser Massage room. "Now here's what we do," said Robin, taking charge. "No sense taking the stairs and all three of us creeping past the concierge's desk. We'll go boldly up in the elevator, each of us pressed against the wall. With luck he'll think the. elevator's going up empty."

Mrs. Pollifax offered him the gun. "Would you like this?"

"No, but I daresay it talks louder than I do." He shoved it into his pocket. "Hafez, what will Serafina do when I knock?"

"She'll ask who's there."

He nodded. "Be sure and tell me if she says anything else." He reached out and ruffled Hafez's jet black hair. "You're quite a lad, Hafez, your father must be damned proud of you."

The elevator carried them past the night porter and up to the third floor. Here they tiptoed down the hall to room 150 and Robin gently tapped on the door.

There were muted footsteps and then a low voice. *"Meen?"*

"She asks who you are," whispered Hafez.

In a thick voice Robin grunted, "Sabry."

The door opened a few inches and Serafina's face peered out. Quickly Robin placed his foot inside and leaned against the door. Serafina's obsequious smile vanished, she gaped in horror, then turned to flee. Robin seized her, placed a hand across the mouth and dragged her to a chair. "I say—someone bring me a curtain cord and a gag. Hurry, she's slippery as an eel."

Hafez produced both. Robin gagged her and then wound the cord round and round her and under the chair as well. "Not bad," he said in a pleased voice. "One could become accustomed to this sort of thing. Now what?"

"I think we move Madame Parviz to my room while I telephone the police," decided Mrs. Pollifax. "I don't like this room, it's not safe."

Robin said, "I couldn't agree with you more." He joined Hafez by the bed and looked curiously at the slender figure lying there unconscious. "So this is the mysterious Madame Parviz. Not quite the dragon I imagined, she looks more like a fallen eagle. Well, steady does it." He lifted her slight body easily. "If someone will open the door—"

She was carried down the hall to Mrs. Pollifax's room

and placed on the bed. Mrs. Pollifax put down the suitcase
with a grateful sigh and then remembered that its contents
were still a mystery and turned to Robin. "Open it," she
said.

"Now?"

"Now."

He took one look at her face, sighed and brought out
his pocket-sized kit of keys. Carrying the suitcase to the
desk he examined the padlocks and set to work grimly.
The first padlock was quickly removed and discarded.
"The second's a combination lock. Be very quiet while I
listen for clicks. Look, can't you be calling the police while
I do this?"

"In a minute," she said impatiently.

The second padlock was removed and Robin bent over
the conventional lock. It snapped, and with a grunt of
triumph he opened the suitcase. Sand-like grains of filler
spilled across the desk. The suitcase was lined with small
plastic sacks of the stuff, some of which had split open
during the jolts of the night. Puzzled, Mrs. Pollifax reached
down and pushed them aside to discover a layer of shredded newspapers. She peeled this away and suddenly
stepped back in horror.

"What on earth?" exclaimed Robin.

"But what is it?" whispered Hafez.

Mrs. Pollifax was staring incredulously at the contents
of the suitcase, at two innocent-looking drab cans suspended in a birdcage-like contraption and placed in a nest
of newspaper and cotton. She had seen two such cans before but when she had seen them they were projected on
the wall of a room in the Hotel Taft in New York. There
was a world of difference between phantoms on a wall and
the real and tangible thing. She could not remember when
she had felt so shocked. She said in a shaken voice, "It's
plutonium—I've just found the plutonium."

The intrigues of Sabry and the sheik abruptly took a
dark and ominous turn and she was caught breathless and

frightened by it. She had the stricken sensation of one who has taken time out to catch a minnow and has unexpectedly reeled in a whale.

Seventeen

"I must telephone," she said in a dazed voice.

Hafez leaned over the suitcase looking awed. "This is PU-239?"

"Don't touch it!" she said sharply. "Not without gloves."

"But it belongs to the *sheik!*" pointed out Robin, reading the label.

"Yes. Astonishing, isn't it?" She was remembering how Marcel had deplored her interest in an old woman and a boy, reminding her that they couldn't possibly be involved in the search for plutonium, and she recalled, too, her reply: of course not, but there is something peculiar there. They had each of them been blind; the two puzzles had always been one and she was incredulous at how easily they fitted together.

She replaced the shreds of newspaper, the sacks of filler and headed for the door with the suitcase. "I'm going downstairs and call the police and then Mr. Carstairs in America. I shall never make the night porter understand unless I'm face to face with him."

"I'll go with you," said Robin.

"Me, too," echoed Hafez.

Ignoring the elevator Mrs. Pollifax hurried down the flight of stairs to the Reception floor with Robin and Hafez in her wake. The night porter rose to his feet, looking startled at such an exodus. "Madame?"

"I want you to put through two telephone calls for me," she said. "First to the police, and then—"

"Police?"

"Police," she repeated firmly.

He shrugged. Dropping a colored envelope on the desk in front of her he moved to the switchboard and plugged into the board. Mrs. Pollifax glanced at her watch—it was nearly 6:30—and then at the envelope. She discovered that it was addressed to her and she opened it, bringing out a cablegram that had arrived for her during the night. She read:

URGENTLY REQUEST KNOWLEDGE CONCERNING CABLE SENT IN MY NAME SUNDAY STOP UNCLE BILL ON THE LOOSE IN FRANCE STOP WHERE IS COUSIN MATTHEW STOP ARE YOU RUNNING A TEMPERATURE STOP LOVE ADELAIDE.

Her immediate reaction was one of intense gratitude— at least *someone* guessed that something was wrong—but since Carstairs was several thousand miles removed from her this was of small comfort. Where were Marcel's people? She had just found Uncle Bill, and she had already found Cousin Matthew if only someone would come to the Clinic and ask. She glanced impatiently at the porter, who was swearing in Italian into the mouthpiece. "Are you speaking with the police?" she asked.

He shook his head. With a bewildered look he removed the headpiece and turned to her. "The line—she is dead."

"Line?"

"Switchboard." He stood up and moved to the rear of the board, checking knobs and outlets. "Dead," he repeated in surprise.

A chill crawled up Mrs. Pollifax's spine. Turning to Robin she met his equally startled gaze. She said quietly, "Try the lights."

There were no light switches at hand; Robin turned instead to the elevator and pushed the button. Nothing happened. No lights twinkled on the board overhead, there was no whispering of descending cables. The elevator, too, was dead.

They're coming, she thought, *they're on their way,* and she drew a deep breath to calm her skidding heart.

Hafez tugged at her arm. "Madame—it cannot be coincidence, surely?"

"I don't know." To the night porter she said, "Does this happen often?"

He sucked in his lower lip judiciously. "In the winter, two or three times, madame. Sometimes. In summer, only with the storm, but—" He shook his head. "No, no, fantastic."

"Where is the director of the Clinic? Can you call him?"

There had to be a director, even if she had not seen him, but after a few skirmishes with the porter's clumsy English it became apparent why she had not seen him. His family was on holiday in France, and he had left Thursday night to bring them back today. The secretary was in charge but she lived in Villeneuve.

Mrs. Pollifax found herself remembering the aerial view of Montbrison that Carstairs had projected on the wall of the Hotel Taft. The Clinic was surrounded by woods, isolated and alone in the center of seventy acres of forest and ravine, its narrow gardens carved out of the hillside with only the one road entering the property from the village a mile away. It would be very easy to lay siege to it. "There are only three of them," she reminded herself aloud.

"Four if you count the sheik," said Robin grimly. "And don't say 'only' four. It's like saying there are 'only' four copperhead snakes on the loose in a small room. I say, if we lock all the doors in the building—"

"With so many windows?" She pulled a memo pad from her purse and began writing. "Robin—" Handing him the slip of paper she said, "One person ought to be able to get away. Don't take your car, go by the path down the mountain and after you've called the police, telephone this number in Baltimore."

"And leave you here alone?" he said incredulously.

"I'm scarcely alone."

"You might just as well be. If they've succeeded in cutting the wires then they'll put up a roadblock and walk in the front door and—"

"Making it all the more important that you get help, Robin!" When he still hesitated she added fiercely, "Have you forgotten Madame Parviz—and Hafez—and the suitcase?"

He sighed. "All right." He pocketed the memo and gave Hafez a tap on the shoulder. "Take over, friend," he said and raced down the stairs to the ground floor and the exit into the gardens.

Mrs. Pollifax turned to Hafez. "Go upstairs to my room and stay with your grandmother, Hafez."

"But you, madame?"

"I've something important to do first. Have you still the toy flashlight in your pocket? I want to borrow it."

Wordlessly he handed it over to her.

"I want you to lock yourself into the room with your grandmother. Lock everything and let no one in, you understand?"

"Very clearly, madame." His eyes were anxious but she saw a glint of excitement in them as he turned and raced up the stairs.

Mrs. Pollifax picked up the suitcase, walked to the stairs and descended to the basement floor. Turning to the right she opened the door marked LABORATORIES and entered the X-ray room. After opening and closing several drawers and cabinets she found what she wanted: a pair of surgeon's gloves. Carrying them and the suitcase she walked down the hall to the storeroom, closed the door and turned on the flashlight. With Hafez's pocket knife she ripped a corner off a carton labeled peaches and then a corner from a carton labeled tomato juice. She studied them critically and then opened up the suitcase to observe its contents.

Drawing on her gloves she cautiously removed the two cans of plutonium from the suitcase, and then from the fragile cages into which they had been inserted. After carrying them carefully to the darkest corner of the supply room she dragged a sack of charcoal in front of them to conceal them and then returned to the cans of fruit. Clearly the cans of peaches were the proper size but each was adorned with a paper label bearing a garish picture. She began to chip away the labels with the pocket knife. This took time. From the kitchen she could hear sounds of movement, an occasional voice and then someone whistling *Marlene*. After a few minutes, deploring the time this was taking—the labels appeared to have been cemented to the tins—she carried them into the X-ray room and dropped them into a sink she filled with water. Alternately scraping and cutting she at last removed all but the smallest fragments. Returning to the store room she rubbed down their shining exteriors with charcoal, inserted them into the cages, packed both cans in the suitcase and replaced the filler and newspapers. Finished, she disposed of the gloves in a wastebasket and hurried upstairs with the suitcase.

There was no one at the concierge's desk. She passed it and hurried up the next flight to her own floor, glancing at her watch as she went. She had been downstairs for fifteen minutes—far too long—but the third level was quiet. No waiters had intruded yet on its silence with trays, and there were no sounds of conversation in the nurse's room.

The electrical failure had interrupted the quiet, unchanging routine.

She turned the corner and abruptly stopped, one hand at her throat. The door to her room stood open. She was so astonished—Hafez had promised to lock it—that she forgot caution and hurried toward it without hesitation.

The room was empty. Madame Parviz no longer lay across the bed. The curtains had been opened and the door to the balcony stood wide. There was no sign of Hafez.

"Hafez?" she whispered, and then, "Hafez!" Moving to the balcony she leaned over the railing and looked down into the garden. "Hafez?" she called.

She turned and hurried down the hall to room 150 and opened the still-unlocked door. Serafina remained bound to the chair, her eyes screaming silent hatred at her. Mrs. Pollifax absently patted her shoulder as she passed her to search the other two rooms. There was no sign of Hafez, or even of Munir and Fouad. If Sabry and his two men were not in the Clinic then why had Hafez bolted, and where had he taken his grandmother? *What had happened while she was in the Clinic basement?*

She ran back to the staircase.

"Good morning," said Court cheerfully, descending from the floor above, "You're certainly up early. There's something wrong with the elevator, have you noticed?"

"Yes. Have you seen Hafez?"

"No, I haven't. Is something wrong?"

But Mrs. Pollifax had already placed one hand on the banister and was hurrying down the stairs to the Reception floor. In her haste she caught the heel of one shoe in the carpet and kept her balance only by dropping the suitcase and clinging with both hands to the railing. The suitcase bumped and slid ahead of her and was retrieved by the head concierge, who had just started up the stairs. "Madame—you are all right?" he called.

She nodded and slipped back into her shoe.

"I was just coming up to knock on your door," he said. "Madame, there are two policemen here inquiring for you."

"Thank heaven," she said, walking down the stairs.

"They would like for you to go with them to the headquarters. A small passport misunderstanding, I am sure."

"Passport misunderstanding?" She stopped on the bottom stair, her eyes on the backs of the two men in uniform standing in the hall and she did not like those two backs at all. Taking a step backward she said, "Where's Robin? Where's Mr. Burke-Jones?"

One of the policemen slowly turned. It was Fouad, looking very continental in uniform. "Good morning, madame," he said pleasantly.

"Good morning," said Munir, walking swiftly to her side.

Mrs. Pollifax turned but it was already too late; each of them held her by an arm. "But these aren't policemen!" she cried to the head concierge. "Don't you recognize them? They came with Madame Parviz, they belong in room 154!"

The head concierge looked startled. "Madame?"

"I said they're not *policemen!*" she cried. "Surely you've seen them before, they came with Madame Parviz! Help me!" she called to Court, who stood transfixed on the staircase.

Gently but firmly Fouad and Munir were pushing her ahead of them to the main door. "Help—help!" cried Mrs. Pollifax as the pressure on her arms mounted. The head concierge gaped at her so blankly that she was forced to remember Fouad and Munir had never stirred from their rooms. "Please!" she gasped, and then as they reached the door she turned and shouted to Court, "They're *not* the police—get help!" For just a moment she succeeded in grasping the knob of the door and hung there, sending a last desperate glance at Court, who stood baffled and uncertain at the foot of the stairs. Then Fouad and Munir lifted her over the threshold and she was carried beyond it, down steps and up the driveway toward two cars that were blocking the entrance.

The sheik jumped out of the nearer car, looking relieved. "Was it necessary to use my name?"

"La," said Fouad.

"Isri."

They carried her, still struggling, past the small car—it was a red Volkswagen—and Mrs. Pollifax glanced inside and with a sinking heart recognized the figure collapsed on the rear seat: it was Madame Parviz. She was picked up again and hurried along to the black Rolls-Royce. Her hands were pushed behind her back, roped painfully together, and then she was shoved inside so roughly that she fell across the trousered legs of the man already occupying the back seat. There was something familiar about those trousers—they were purple, she saw in dismay—and as she was plucked from the floor by unseen hands and hurled into the seat Robin said grimly, "They caught me, too—about five feet from the edge of the garden. A bloody rout, I'd say."

Eighteen

After leaving Mrs. Pollifax down-stairs in the hall, Hafez had gone up to her room and locked himself inside with his grandmother. He had also locked the door to the balcony and drawn the heavy curtains. When he heard the footsteps in the hall he was sitting quietly beside the bed. He might not even have no-

ticed them except that the steps paused at Mrs. Pollifax's
door and a board creaked. Hafez stood up to face the
door, expecting at any moment to hear Mrs. Pollifax call,
"Hafez?"

But Mrs. Pollifax did not call. The quilted outer door
was drawn softly open and he watched the knob of the
locked inner door turn slowly to the right and then to the
left. His heart hammering, he moved back to stand beside
his grandmother. He heard a low, sibilant whisper and
words spoken in Arabic. "It's locked. Hand over the skel-
eton key."

It was Fouad at the door.

Hafez's heart thudded so violently that he thought it
must surely burst through his shirt. "Grandmama," he
whispered, but his grandmother did not stir. He began to
search for a weapon—anything, a pair of scissors, a paperweight—but there was nothing at hand. He thought of
the pockets of his windbreaker jacket but he already knew
their contents: several inches of rope, his tape recorder
and spare tapes, a pencil and a few exotic stones collected
for their color but not their weight. As the key rattled in
the lock he backed farther and farther from the bed until
he reached the door to the balcony and stood pressed
against it. He realized with an acute sense of grief that he
was going to have to abandon his grandmother. He had no
alternative, it was either leave or be taken by these men
and, if taken, there might be no hope at all for either of
them.

He slipped behind the curtains, tugged at the door and
stepped out on the balcony just as the door to Mrs. Pollifax's room opened. As the two men walked inside he
climbed over the railing onto the ledge. The adjacent
balcony was unoccupied and he crouched there a moment
out of sight, trying to think how to escape. There were
many exits on the ground floor but there was no way of
reaching any of them without passing the concierge's desk.
Robin had gone for the police. The important thing was to

find out what Fouad and Munir planned to do with his grandmother so that he could inform the police when they arrived. He had to find a way to keep an eye on the two men without being seen himself.

In his eight days at the Clinic Hafez had followed the code of every ten-year-old: he had explored all the corners and unmarked rooms that adults accepted as out-of-bounds or of no interest at all. Now he recalled the dumbwaiter in the utility closet next to room 148 and he wondered if he could reach it without being noticed. He cautiously made his way along the ledge. At this hour there was no one in the garden below, and apparently the occupants of the rooms he edged past were still asleep. He reached the balcony of room 154 and climbed over the railing. The door stood open and he walked through the room to the hall door and peered out. The corridor was empty. Taking a deep breath he raced down the hall and ducked inside the utility room. Opening the door of the dumbwaiter he tugged at the ropes and brought the box up to the third floor, climbed inside and began to lower himself hand over hand. It reminded him of the chute at the Castle de Chillon and he remembered Mrs. Pollifax saying that they must be resourceful.

Well, he thought, they had been resourceful at the castle and they had not been caught. Now it was up to him to be even cleverer because he was alone.

There were voices in the kitchen, waiters grumbling over the loss of electricity and the tediousness of a wood-burning stove. The dumbwaiter reached the bottom of the shaft and Hafez pushed open the door, stared at three startled faces and climbed out. *"Bon jour,"* he said brightly, and walked past them to the door and outside into the maze of trellises that concealed the exit. This brought him to the greenhouse and he ducked around it, climbed the high bank to the road, ran across the road and took refuge in a clump of bushes from which he could see the front door.

He hoped it was the front door that he should watch.

He stared at the walls of the Clinic, thinking of all the people inside asleep but this only made him feel lonely. Even if they were awake, he thought, they wouldn't know, and if by some chance they learned what was happening they wouldn't *believe*. It was the first time he had understood that a conspiracy existed among the living to wall out and reject what was disturbing. It took special people like Mrs. Pollifax and Robin to understand, he thought, and he supposed it was because they were in someway outsiders. They had stepped out of the circle long enough to see the shadows. They had dared the loneliness.

He felt a wave of infinite gratitude toward them and he thought, "I will be like them when I grow up, I swear I will."

A movement at Sabry's window caught his eye. He saw the balcony door open and Fouad walk out, peer to his left in the direction of the road and then wave a hand. A moment later Sheik Yazdan ibn Kazdan strolled down the driveway and entered the Clinic. Several minutes later Fouad and Munir stumbled out of the door carrying his grandmother. They were obviously in a great hurry, which meant they must barely have made it past the concierge's desk without being discovered. This was something the sheik must have arranged.

Where are the police, wondered Hafez impatiently.

The two men with their burden walked up the driveway past the greenhouse. As they came abreast of Hafez in his hiding place he ducked his head and began to move with them parallel to the road, taking care to walk carefully. At the top of the incline he saw two cars blocking the Clinic's entrance drive, one a small red Volkswagen, the other a long black Rolls-Royce. Sabry emerged from the latter and helped the two men place Madame Parviz inside the Volkswagen. The three then stood beside the car, talking and smoking.

Hafez had no paper but he did have a pencil. He drew it

out, wet it with his lips and tested it on the inside of his nylon windbreaker. It wrote, and he carefully copied down on his jacket the license numbers of the two cars. He had scarcely finished doing this when the sheik came out of the Clinic. He and the three men began an argument, during which Hafez heard his name spoken several times, and then Fouad and Munir stripped off their jackets and stepped behind the cars. When they reappeared Hafez saw that they wore uniforms of some kind. The sheik opened the trunk of the Rolls and tossed their old clothes inside.

Why didn't the police come, Hafez thought desperately. He watched Fouad and Munir walk down the driveway in their matching uniforms and he guessed they were going into the Clinic now to find Madame Pollifax. There was no reason to believe they wouldn't capture her, too, and then he would be the only one left.

He would be the only one who knew—but what could he give Robin and the police except the license numbers of two cars that might have already vanished by the time they came? It was not enough.

He had seen the sheik open the trunk of the Rolls and toss clothes inside. It was a large trunk, and he knew it was unlocked. Now the sheik had climbed inside the car and he and Sabry sat talking in the front seat. It was very quiet except for the low murmur of their voices and birds chattering in the tall trees.

We have to be resourceful, Madam Pollifax had said.

Hafez moved swiftly. Once behind the Volkswagen he slid to his knees and crawled around it to the back of the Rolls and crouched there. Ever so gently he lifted the door to the trunk and opened it half way. It creaked a little but the murmur of voices continued. Climbing inside he lowered it softly behind him and stuffed a corner of Fouad's jacket into the opening to leave a crack for fresh air.

Nineteen

When the sheik's car reached the village

it did not turn to the left to head down the mountain, it turned to the right to begin a precipitous climb upward. Mrs. Pollifax looked at the sheik seated opposite her on the jump seat and said, "Where are we going?"

His dark eyes were friendly as he smiled. "In due time we separate. I go far, madame, but you and the other two will go no farther than I wish you to go. You have been, you know, a very naughty lady."

That sounded patronizing and she told him so.

His eyebrows lifted. "How so? You have been only a minor inconvenience, no more than a buzzing gnat. Can one give to a gnat obeisance or importance?"

"I can't speak for Mrs. Pollifax," said Robin, "but I resent being called a gnat and a minor inconvenience, damn it."

The sheik laughed. "Well said, Burke-Jones, I'd feel the same way myself. Your face is familiar to me, by the way. Have we met?"

"Paris—'65," Robin said shortly. "Le Comte de Reuffe's weekend party. Gabrielle's ball. The races at Deauville."

"Ah yes, I remember now. Have you news of them? . . . '65 was a gay year, it lingers in my mind like vintage wine on the palate. I understand that Jackie has married?"

"Twice since then," said Robin.

Mrs. Pollifax only half-listened. She was looking around

her as the road narrowed and the houses thinned. They were moving now up a steep slope through thick dark woods, they rounded a curve and suddenly they were at the top of the mountain on which Montbrison rested. But this peak was negligible, no more than a foothill, a steppingstone to what lay beyond, for they were surrounded by even higher peaks that merged into other, taller mountains stretching ahead like an endless cyclorama. Patches of forest broke up the quilt pattern here and there, and each seam of green on these lower slopes boasted a small village or cluster of chalets. Far off on another rock projection Mrs. Pollifax could see a tiny train chugging along like a slug, its smoke almost transparent against the pale blue sky.

"No, I can't believe that," Robin was saying. "Really I can't. Gabrielle a nun? I thought she married Roger."

It was too civilized for Mrs. Pollifax. "Where are we going?" she asked again.

"No, no, it was Danielle who married Roger," protested the sheik.

This name reminded Mrs. Pollifax of the film on Saturday evening—the heroine's name had been Danielle—and this in turn reminded her of Hafez, who had promised to confide the plot to her and had never done so. She realized that she was very frightened for him because he had been guarding his grandmother, and Madame Parviz was in the car behind them. What had happened to him? She recalled her impressions of the back seat of the Volkswagen and what she had seen in that quick glance inside. There had been only the one crumpled figure with head against the window and eyes closed . . . but if they had found Madame Parviz they must have found Hafez, too and he was not in the Volkswagen. If they had killed him— "Where is Hafez?" she demanded.

The sheik turned to look at her with interest. "Hafez?" He shrugged. "I don't think we need to worry about Hafez."

"I should like to worry," she told him.

Again he shrugged, this time with a pleasant smile. "But Hafez is—shall we say, expendable?" Over his shoulder he called, "Ibrahim, are we nearly there?"

"We are nearly there, Sayyid."

Expendable, thought Mrs. Pollifax, and felt a little sick.

They had been climbing all the time and now they had reached a bald, wind-swept plateau which ran like a spine across the mountain they'd left to the mountain ahead. Patches of thin grass grew wherever they found a little earth but there was little earth that had not been swept away by the winds. Mrs. Pollifax looked out of the car window and down, and caught a glimpse of Lake Geneva far, far below. The car slowed, and up ahead she saw a seam in the stony earth, a narrow cart track winding off toward the stony knob of a hill to the right. The car turned off the paved road and jolted and leaped across the ground with the Volkswagen following behind them.

They approached the knoll on a bias, winding around boulders and fields of dead earth littered with pebbles. There were no trees, they must be too high for trees, decided Mrs. Pollifax, and she began to feel the total hopelessness of their situation. It would be better to take each moment as it came, she told herself, and acknowledged for the first time that not many moments might lie ahead.

The car cleared the knob of the hill and Mrs. Pollifax looked ahead and saw a chalet, a weatherbeaten, closed-up Alpine cottage perched absurdly up here among the rocks and the clouds, its shuttered windows overlooking what must be a spectacular view of the country miles below. A single stunted tree was its only companion. As she watched, a cloud of mist drifted lazily toward them across the stony meadow. It obliterated the gnarled old tree, stroked the chalet with long ghost-like fingers and then swirled toward them. A moment later it had surrounded the car, damp and sunless and gray. When they emerged from its clutch the car had reached the chalet.

Robin peered out. "I say, this doesn't seem up to your standards as a *pied-à-terre,*" he said, still playing the *bon vivant.*

"This?" said the sheik, startled. "Oh my dear fellow, this was rented only last evening when it became apparent that you and your friend were becoming nuisances. A pity, too, for it amused me to use the Clinic."

"Amused you?" said Robin.

"It's so much more dangerous," he explained simply. "There was the irony of it, too. I happen to be a member of the Board of Directors, you see. I am so very welcome there."

I don't think we're going to get out of this, thought Mrs. Pollifax bleakly, and turned her head as the Volkswagen pulled up beside them. Fouad climbed out and went up the steps of the chalet to unlock the door. With the door open he waved them in. The sheik uncrossed his long legs and stepped out of the car. "Sabry?"

Sabry nodded and brought out a gun. "You will go inside the chalet," he told them without expression.

Robin climbed out first, and as he turned to face her for the first time she saw that the right side of his face was scratched and torn, and his right eye swollen almost closed. "Oh Robin," she said sadly.

"I've obviously lived much too sedentary a life," he said lightly. "A fact that I intend to rectify at the earliest possible moment if I ever get out of this in one piece." His hands were also tied but as she climbed out he succeeded in lifting them to touch her arm reassuringly. At the moment it only made her want to cry.

They moved across the rocks to the wooden steps. Mrs. Pollifax turned for one last look around her but the empty, windswept landscape was so distressingly bleak that she did not linger; she entered the chalet almost gratefully.

Inside it was midnight, every window shuttered and barred. Fouad was lighting an oil lamp and as it flared up to illuminate the room he looked at her once, briefly, and she saw the hate in his eyes. Then he lifted the lamp and carried it to a table in the middle of the room, his face impassive.

"Cheerless place," said Robin behind her. "Rather like a cottage at Brighton in the off season."

It was precisely what it did resemble; it still held within it the bone-chilling damp of winter, the furnishings were shabby and dusty and the grate in the fireplace empty. There was a strong smell of cooking oil and mothballs.

"Planning to stay long?" quipped Robin.

The sheik moved away from the door as Munir carried in Madame Parviz and lowered her, none too gently, to the couch in front of the fireplace. Because Sabry chose this moment to glance at his watch, Mrs. Pollifax glanced at hers too; it was eight o'clock, which was difficult to realize in this lightless room. Sabry and the sheik began talking amiably in Arabic. The sheik brought out his wallet, counted an enormous number of Swiss francs into Sabry's palm and wished him well. Sabry went out, closing the door behind him.

"I wish I knew where he's going," Mrs. Pollifax said to Robin in a low voice. "I wish Hafez were here to translate that for us."

The sheik heard her and smiled. "But I have no secrets from you," he said, his eyes twinkling at her. "Ibrahim has gone to bring back a helicopter. You may have noticed that the terrain here is quite suitable for its landing. I've no intention of lingering any longer in Switzerland and since I've no idea what little hints either of you may have left behind at the Clinic I shall proceed as if the Clinic—as if all of Switzerland!—is looking for me." He appeared delighted at the thought. "To outwit them—oh superb sport, that."

"You're quite a sportsman," Robin said dryly.

"But of course—I am a Bedouin," he said with dignity. "Sit down, there is no need to stand on ceremony. The chairs are dusty but far more comfortable than standing. Munir—we'll have food now."

Mrs. Pollifax lowered herself into a straight chair near the fireplace, her tied wrists extended awkwardly in front of her. Across the room she met Robin's gaze and recognized the question in his eyes. She spoke it aloud. "What do you plan to do with us—with Robin, Madame Parviz and me?"

The sheik walked to the fireplace and rested a hand on the mantel. "I'm sorry you ask," he said regretfully. "I thought we could enjoy a rather charming picnic here together while we wait. It may be a wait of several hours and unfortunately—" He sighed. "Unfortunately Fouad and Munir have never developed the art of conversation. They remain distressingly utilitarian." He sighed. "In such bleak surroundings a little conversation helps to smooth the passing of time. Surely we need not discuss such a painful thing as your futures?"

"They are," pointed out Mrs. Pollifax, *"our* futures."

"Were," he corrected gently, with a smile. "Now of course they belong to me. We have a proverb that says 'If you are a peg, endure the knocking; if you are a mallet, strike.' I hope that you will endure with fortitude the consequences of your meddling."

"Haven't you been doing a little meddling of your own?" inquired Mrs. Pollifax.

He laughed. "It is all in the eye of the beholder, is it not? However, to answer your question as tactfully as possible, let me say that the helicopter, when it arrives, will have no room for you and Mr. Burke-Jones. There will be space only for Fouad, Munir, Ibrahim, myself and Madame Parviz, who—as you may have guessed—is still of some importance as a hostage. Now please, let us say no more, it becomes distasteful to me. There are always a few who have to be sacrificed for the greater good. We also have a saying 'What is brought by the wind will be carried away by the wind.' Ah, good—good," he said happily as Munir came in carrying firewood.

Quickly and efficiently Munir arranged the wood in the fireplace and lighted a fire. Once it was ignited he spread a rug on the floor in front of it—a gorgeous Persian rug, Mrs. Pollifax noted—and distributed cushions around it. Incense was placed on the mantel, a match applied to it and the scent of sandalwood met her nostrils. Then Munir retired to the kitchen off to the left and the rattle of cups could be heard. Mrs. Pollifax stood up and walked over to the fire, holding her bound hands out to warm them but it was uncomfortable standing so near the sheik and she retreated to the couch and sat down at the end of it, near Madame Parviz's feet. The poor woman was still unconscious, her eyes closed, but a second later Mrs. Pollifax glanced again at her and was not so sure. She thought a gleam of light showed between the fringe of her lashes and the bone of her cheek. She did not look again.

"For the greater good of what?" she asked the sheik. "If we're to be so lightly sacrificed perhaps you can tell us the great benefit the world is going to gain?"

"The benefits are Allah's, I am only the instrument," he told her sternly.

Munir returned carrying a tray. On it were tiny cups and a large, beak-nosed brass coffeepot which exuded a spicy fragrance and a cloud of steam. The fire flickered across the rug, picking out its jewel-like colors and the patina of brass. A dusty Brighton cottage was rapidly turning into an Arab tent, she thought, and she couldn't help but admire this imposing of will upon a shell of a house.

Robin said stiffly, "If you're planning to feed us—in the interest of fascinating conversation—we can't possibly manage with our hands tied."

"Quite so," the sheik said amiably. "They will be untied once Munir has completed his chores." With a twinkle for

Mrs. Pollifax he added, "But you will please notice that Fouad is at the door with his gun."

She had already noticed him squatting by the door in the shadows; she took note and glanced away. "These plans you have," she said to the sheik, looking at him steadily. "You're responsible for the death of Marcel and you're responsible for the death of a man named Fraser, and now you would kill us as well. This is what you call being the instrument of Allah?"

He shrugged. "In war many people are killed, men and women, children, soldiers, and onlookers. But I am surprised that you know about Fraser. How is this?"

Robin, too, was watching her curiously. "You can't possibly mean the English chap who was injured at the Clinic last week! Do you mean he was murdered?" he asked the sheik, turning to him. "And it had something to do with you?"

The sheik smiled. "He was a professional British agent, my dear Burke-Jones. Unfortunately most of his work had been done in the Middle East so that he and Ibrahim had met before. So long as Ibrahim convalesced quietly and took the sun there was no harm in sharing the Clinic. But of course once the Parvizes arrived the situation would have been intolerable. Fraser would have guessed something was up at once. He had to be removed."

Robin thought about this for a moment and then said coolly, "I happen to be a British agent, too, you know, and since Mrs. Pollifax has absolutely nothing to do with any of this I insist that you let her go at once."

Before Mrs. Pollifax could protest this wasted act of galantry the sheik laughed. "I don't believe you for a moment, Burke-Jones, and I couldn't possibly allow her to go free. It's she, after all, who was found in Ibrahim's room. She knows too much. Enough of such nonsense." As Munir poured coffee from the pot into tiny cups he said, "Have you tasted *herisa* before? It's an herb coffee, I think you'll enjoy it. Munir, you may cut their ropes now. It is better there be no marks on their wrists."

No marks on the bodies, thought Mrs. Pollifax, and as a second tray was brought in bearing pastries and dates she experienced an almost hysterical urge to laugh. A Persian rug, tiny cups of herb coffee, incense, and a sheik—it was too much. She controlled her wild upsurge of laughter and abruptly felt like bursting into tears. "You travel with originality," she managed to say.

The sheik flashed his white smile at her. "We have a proverb, 'He who has money can eat sherbet in hell.' Anything is possible with money."

"Including the buying of armies and lives?" she said tartly. She held up her wrists to Munir, who carefully severed the bonds around her wrists, and when he had done this she rubbed them, wincing. But she could eat now, and she was grateful.

The sheik paused with his cup halfway to his lips and smiled. "Only a means to an end, Mrs. Pollifax. You spoke of meddling. Your meddling is destructive—it's in my way—but mine is constructive."

"In what way?"

"You have a saying, 'They shall beat their swords into plowshares.' " He turned his face to her, his eyes remote. "A rabble of men cannot do this, they are insufficiently enlightened but one man can accomplish what has never been accomplished before. I shall bring peace to the world, to the entire world."

"If only you could," she said longingly. "But bloodlessly?"

He smiled. "We have a saying that first it is necessary to build up the inside of the mosque and then the outside. No, not bloodlessly, because men are children and must have their quarrels."

Mrs. Pollifax sighed. "I should have guessed not."

"It will be a quick bloodletting, though. I have my own army in the desert, you see, they have been training secretly for some time, as well as collecting other certain—uh—instruments of power. I have scientists, a laboratory, munitions, all hidden away in the desert. All that is lacking now is a country, a base, but it is astonishing how easy it all is. In this materialistic world men will sell their souls for a few dollars. When one has money one can buy anyone."

"Apparently you couldn't buy King Jarroud," pointed out Mrs. Pollifax.

"Ah, but I have undermined him," he said with the flash of a smile, "and that has been far more enjoyable. General Parviz will be no trouble to me, the road to the throne is wide open." His smile became radiant. "One of the five pillars of the Moslem faith is the people's willingness to participate in *jihad*. Do you know what *jihad* is, madame?"

"A holy war," said Robin in a bleak voice.

"Quite so, yes," said the sheik. "The redress of wrongs is an act of religious obedience in Islam. I have had a vision—Muhammed came to me in a dream one night—telling me that the time has come, and that I am sayyid."

Mrs. Pollifax put down her cup and stared at him, caught by the play of emotion, a look almost of ecstasy on his face. She confessed herself moved by the passion in his voice and the almost hypnotic quality of his words.

"The Moslems have waited a long time," he went on, the fire illuminating the fierce profile and flashing eyes. "Nasser promised hope at first but it was Allah's will that he be struck down. Now Moslems quarrel among themselves. There is Quadaffi and there is Sadat and Hussein and Jarroud and we are all divided but I shall unite us in *jihad*—with one stroke—and when we are truly united we will be soldiers together, and when we have won back what is ours we shall impose peace on the whole world."

"Impose?" There was silence until Mrs. Pollifax, already guessing the answer, said softly, "How?"

"By the means given me to impose it." His smile deepened. "That, dear lady, is too great a secret to divulge but I have the means, never fear, the means to the glorious end promised me by the Prophet Himself. I can assure you the world will pay attention. *Allah Akhbar!*"

From Fouad came a resounding, *"Allah Akhbar!"*

"Your plans include much more than Zabya, then."

He laughed. "Of course. I'm surprised that you didn't see that at once. Zabya?" He shrugged. "A small desert country with a tiresome, idealistic little king. Who could possibly settle for Zabya? For me it shall be the beginning, a base in the center of an oil-rich continent, a foothold, a foundation on which to build an empire. Mohammed himself began with only the town of Medina, yet before he died he had changed millions of people's lives and had given us Mecca. After his death his followers carried Islam as far as France."

"And so you will be the new Alexander," said Mrs. Pollifax quietly.

He leaned forward, his eyes intense. "You must confess —if you consider it honestly and realistically—that what the world needs now—before it destroys itself—is one ruler. One law. One government. It is the only way to survive."

"Good God," put in Robin deflatingly, "you mean one damned bureaucracy to botch things instead of dozens? The red tape staggers the imagination."

The sheik ignored him. "The key to it all—the key to the master stroke—lies in that suitcase," he said abruptly. "You see it standing on the table? You broke open the locks but you couldn't possibly understand what you saw. I have already tested myself—myself and my cunning—by making fools of high men all over the world. It has pleased me a great deal. It was my first adventure, my beginning."

This had the effect of cheering Mrs. Pollifax's flagging spirits because she was the only one in the room who knew that he was addressing two cans of peaches instead of a suitcase bearing several kilograms of plutonium.

"You can't possibly succeed, it's too outrageous," Robin said.

The sheik smiled at him benevolently. "A thief is a king until he is caught." He rinsed his fingers in a bowl of water and dried them on a towel that Munir held out to him. Rising he said, "Join me, Munir, it's time." To Fouad he added, "Remain attentive. Keep your distance and shoot if they move."

He and Munir disappeared into another room and she exchanged glances with Robin across the Persian rug. Over by the door, some fifteen feet away. Fouad rose to his feet and leaned against the door, his eyes bored as he watched them. There was silence except for the crackling of the fire until Robin said, "I'm beginning to take him seriously."

"Yes," said Mrs. Pollifax.

"All this business about peace—it doesn't sound very peaceful to me."

"It's the latest style of peace," she said dryly. "It's called waging peace with limited-duration reinforced protective reaction strikes, low kill-ratio and no incursions."

"I see. But not war," said Robin gravely.

"Oh, no, not *war*. Good heavens no."

From the next room the sheik intoned in a powerful voice: *"La ilaha illa llah, Muhammed rasul allah."*

"He's praying," Robin pointed out. "I daresay we should be praying, too. I mean, it does begin to look a bit final, the three of them against the two of us. And when Sabry gets back with a helicopter there'll be four of them. Look, there's something I wanted to mention, not important, I daresay, but something funny about the boot of the car we came in—or trunk, as you Americans call it."

"And something I have to ask you," she told him.

Each stopped, waiting for the other, and in the silence a low voice from the couch between them said, "Not two against four. Three."

Mrs. Pollifax turned to look at Madame Parviz lying there, her eyes closed.

Robin said, "Did she—?"

"Yes," said Mrs. Pollifax.

Lips barely moving and eyes still shut Madame Parviz said, "There is a poker on the hearth."

"We'd better not look at her," Mrs. Pollifax advised Robin.

"A bit of luck having her conscious at last," he pointed out in a low voice. "I'm not sure I can reach the poker without Fouad seeing me. Have you noticed how carefully they keep their distance from us? It's like a planned choreography—downright obvious."

"They're aware that I know some karate," explained Mrs. Pollifax.

"So that's it!" said Robin, brightening. "I must say that until meeting you I seem to have led the most common-place life. You might have told me you knew karate. If that's the case Madame Parviz can be armed with the poker and all we need are some brass knuckles for me. Stay with us, Madame Parviz!"

"But there has to be some way to get near them," pointed out Mrs. Pollifax.

"It's what we've got to wait for," Robin said. "Just one mistake, just one slip and we might be able to jump them. Damn it, I refuse to give up without protest." He was stretching out one leg so that his foot extended across the Persian rug to the hearth. Very carefully he prodded the tip of the poker, and when his foot only pushed it farther away he swore under his breath.

"It's a break not having our hands tied," Mrs. Pollifax pointed out. "How long do you suppose we have?"

"You heard the man, until Sabry brings back the helicopter. It's not hopeless, you know. If we can stall, somehow catch them off balance—"

Stall, mused Mrs. Pollifax, and it occurred to her there might be a way to confuse the sheik and his men, even to persuade them to postpone their escape. If she could say enough but not too much—Aloud she said, "There's one thing I could do that might give us a chance to get nearer them."

"What?"

"I don't think it's wise to tell the sheik we know about the plutonium, do you?"

"Good God, no," said Robin. "Keeping it secret seems to feed his superiority. He'd probably kill us on the spot."

"That's what I felt. But I can tell the sheik I replaced the two cans in the suitcase with two cans of peaches from the Clinic."

The glance Robin gave her was withering. "That's a singularly uninspired idea and not at all up to your usual standards. Do you take him for a fool?"

"But that's exactly—" She stopped as the sheik returned, rubbing his hands together with satisfaction. As he looked from one face to the other they all heard it: the sound of a helicopter's blades beating the air at some distance away. Fouad opened the door. "Sayyid," he said eagerly.

"Allah be praised, he's early. Munir—" He gestured toward the rug. "Pack up our things, we'll be leaving in a few minutes. There's no point in your killing them, Sabry will do it."

The sound of the helicopter filled the room; a gust of air blew in through the open door, lifting ashes from the fireplace and scattering them. The noise abruptly stilled, and a minute later Mrs. Pollifax heard the crunch of shoes on the pebbles outside. Her heart began to hammer sickeningly against her ribs. As Sabry entered the room she stood up and said in a clear loud voice, "I have something to say to you."

Twenty

The sheik glanced at his watch. "*Very*
well—say it, but be quick."

She lifted her head and said steadily, "There are only
cans of peaches in your suitcase."

"I beg your pardon!" he said in astonishment.

"For God's sake," groaned Robin.

Her head went higher. "I think you should know that
just before you brought me here I removed the two original cans and substituted two cans of fruit for them. The
real ones are back at the Clinic."

He looked amused. "Which means that really we should
not kill you yet, is this correct? Instead we should all drive
back to the Clinic and play hide-and-seek again?"

"Whatever you feel necessary," she said calmly. "But I
wanted to stress that if you kill us now you'll be sorry later
for very practical reasons, if not moral ones. You won't
know how to find the original two cans."

"That's very true, of course," he said politely, watching
her face. "Munir," he added briskly, "bring us a can
opener."

"Now you've done it," murmured Robin.

Mrs. Pollifax waited. Munir went into the kitchen and
returned bearing a small metal can opener. "Give it to
her," ordered the sheik.

"Sayyid," said Sabry in protest.

The sheik waved his protest aside. "No, no, this amuses
me, Ibrahim, let us see what she dares."

Munir handed Mrs. Pollifax the can opener and she moved to the table in the center of the room. Opening the suitcase she slowly removed the plastic bags of filler and then the layers of shredded newspaper. She had at least gained the middle of the room, and she hoped that Robin would realize this. Detaching one of the cans from its cage she set it on the table, gripped the handle of the can opener and bent over it.

Abruptly a hand was placed over hers and she looked up into the cold dark eyes of the sheik. "That will be enough," he said curtly. "You are a very good actress and it's a clever trick on your part but do you really believe I would allow you to injure the contents of this can?"

"But it's only a can of peaches," she protested. "How can I persuade you unless I open it?"

"Shoot her, Ibrahim," he said in a bored voice and turned away. "Kill her, she grows tiresome."

"You bloody coward," cried Robin, stepping forward.

"Back!" snarled Ibrahim Sabry, lifting his gun. His sharp command was echoed by a shouted command from outside the chalet and Mrs. Pollifax saw Robin stop in midstride. Everyone stopped, it was like a game of Statues, Robin with one foot off the floor, the sheik with arm lifted, Fouad by the door with his mouth open, Sabry four feet away from her with his gun leveled at her head. And when the scene unfroze, she thought, Robin would place his left foot on the floor, the sheik would lower his hand, Sabry's finger would squeeze the trigger and she would die. The moment felt endless, she wanted to scream, "Get it over with!" and then she realized that what had turned them into stone was that all of the sheik's men were inside this room but the voice had come from outside.

"*Ici la police.——Sortez, les mains en l'air!*" called the voice.

No one moved. The moment stretched out interminably. She stood dazed, not understanding the words and wondering why the voice sounded so familiar, wondering why a picture flashed into her mind of a sunny morning in a garden and an old man leaning on a cane, and then she understood that it was the voice of General d' Estaing that she heard. She thought incredulously, the general *here?*

And then a second voice called, "Come out with your hands high—the jig is up!"

Robin's voice. *Robin's voice on a tape recorder.*

"Hafez," she whispered. He was alive.

"What the devil!" cried the sheik, and at once the spell was broken. Mrs. Pollifax threw herself at Sabry and knocked the gun out of his hand. As the gun clattered to the floor she slashed at him with her other hand and he staggered to the floor. Turning she saw that Robin had hurled himself upon Fouad and was struggling for his gun. As she stepped back Munir ran across the room to pluck Sabry's gun from the floor. He dropped it, bent to pick it up again and she kicked him. He grasped her leg and brought her down to the rug with him and they rolled over. The gun went off and sent a searing hot flame up her left arm. Just as Munir reached for her throat with both hands a figure in a long white robe rushed across the room and hit him over the head with a poker.

Mrs. Pollifax sat up. Her head spinning dizzily and she felt a little sick. Madame Parviz was standing over Fouad and Robin was sitting on the floor brushing dust from his trousers. The sheik was nowhere to be seen, nor was the suitcase. Mrs. Pollifax stumbled to her feet, swayed a little, and made her way to the door.

The sheik was climbing into the helicopter that sat like a bloated dragonfly among the rocks outside. She saw the blades begin to rotate, churn, and then blur, and as she limped to the top step the helicopter lifted from the ground and she and the sheik exchanged a long glance through the Plexiglas window. The helicopter turned, lifted, and soared away over the hill, and as its noise diminished she heard the tape recorder call over and over *the jig is up the jig is up the jig . . .*

She sat down weakly on the top step and said "Hafez?"

The droning mechanical words seemed to come from the solitary tree on the hillside. "Hafez?" she called again, louder.

Hafez emerged from behind the tree. He hesitated until he saw her and then came bounding over the rocks toward her, a small intense figure radiating joy. "Madame!" he cried. "Oh madame, it *worked!*"

"Hafez," she said with feeling, "you've just saved our lives. However did you find us!"

"Find you? But madame, I never left you," he cried happily. "I hid in the trunk of the limousine. Don't you remember you said we must all be resourceful?"

"Resourceful," repeated Mrs. Pollifax, and frowned over a word that sounded familiar to her but held no meaning at all. "Resourceful," she said again, and looked up at the sun which had suddenly begun to skid across the sky.

Hafez gasped. "Madame—there is blood dripping on the stair!" His glance lifted to her arm and his eyes widened in horror. She heard him shout, "Grandmama! Robin! She has been shot!" and then, "Monsieur, she is fainting!"

Someone leaned over her, words were spoken, she was lifted and carried to the car while over and over the tape recorder called out *the jig is up the jig is up the jig is up the jig . . .* In the darkness that followed she heard a strange variety of voices—Bishop's first of all, but that was impossible because Bishop belonged in America—and then she thought she heard General d'Estaing speaking, and Court's reply, and then Dr. Lichtenstein commanded them to be quiet and there was silence. A long black silence.

Twenty-One

Mrs. Pollifax opened her eyes to find that she was lying in bed in her room at Montbrison. She stared at the ceiling, puzzled, and then her glance moved slowly down the wall, which an evening sun had striped with gold, and when her eyes focused on the face of the man seated beside her she said, "Whatever are you doing here!"

Bishop looked up from a magazine and grinned. "Is that any way to welcome me? Good God, when I arrived this morning I thought I'd arrived in time for your funeral. Carstairs sent me. He had a strong hunch things were going wrong."

She said dreamily, "They went wrong for me in the right way. Or right for me in the wrong way." She frowned. "Why do I feel so peculiar, Bishop?"

"You've just had a bullet removed from your arm," he explained. "You were bleeding like hell so Dr. Lichtenstein gave you a whiff of something and removed it in his office. They don't have an operating room here."

"Oh," she said, and tried to make sense of his explanation, which seemed very odd to her until she peered at her arm and discovered it swathed in gauze and bound to a splint.

"It's still Monday—only seven o'clock in the evening," he assured her. "Interpol has been here all day putting the pieces together and worrying like hell about you. They found a woman tied to a chair in room 150, and Marcel's body in the closet of room 153. I take it you've had a rather busy weekend?"

"Yes," she said, looking back on it from a vast distance and then the distance abruptly telescoped and she struggled to sit up. "The sheik?"

Bishop shook his head. "He got away. His private plane took off from Geneva airport at twelve noon."

"But the *coup d'etat*—?"

"Firmly squashed—we *think*—but here's Schoenbeck," Bishop said, rising. "He's the man who can tell you about it. Mrs. Pollifax, it's high time you meet Henri Schoenbeck of Interpol."

Monsieur Schoenbeck advanced into the room looking a little shy, a little prim, his lips pursed but his eyes warm as they encountered hers. "And I, madame, am in your debt," he said, giving her a long and searching glance as he grasped her right hand. He returned it gently to her bed. "It is my loss that we meet only now, madame."

"Are you the person to whom I signaled?" she asked.

"No, no, that was Gervard." His lips curved faintly into a smile. "It may amuse you, madame, to learn that after allowing you to become settled at Montbrison over the weekend we had planned to pay a call upon you today and set up a more suitable contact. We had wanted," he explained, "to give you the weekend to become oriented. A plan, I might add, that has nearly cost you your life."

"Well," said Mrs. Pollifax politely, "it all appears to be over now, so there scarcely seems any point in post-mortems."

"Then allow me to tell you that I have just returned from the chalet on the Wildehorn. Burke-Jones and Hafez accompanied me, and on the way they told me a great deal of what happened. It may console you to learn that at this moment the sheik's three men are entering a nearby prison."

"It consoles me," she admitted, "but the sheik has flown away, I hear, with his peaches?"

Schoenbeck frowned. "I beg your pardon?"

"With the peaches."

Schoenbeck and Bishop exchanged glances. "Probably the chloroform," suggested Bishop.

Schoenbeck nodded. "The head becomes light." He said gently, "There is no need to pretend any longer now, madame. I have been told that you tried to persuade the sheik that he did not have the plutonium but you are quite safe now, you know."

Mrs. Pollifax sighed. "I suppose there *is* something absurd about peaches, Monsieur Schoenbeck, but I can assure you that what I said was true. The plutonium never left the Clinic. It's here."

"I think I believe her," said Bishop in an astonished voice.

"Never left the Clinic!" echoed Schoenbeck. "But then the French consignment—the French plutonium—is no longer in the hands of the sheik? Madame, if you would tell me precisely where it is—"

Mrs. Pollifax ignored the question and instead smiled at him dazzlingly. "What do you think of Robin, Monsieur Schoenbeck?"

"Robin? He has surprised me, that much I will say."

"If you mean Burke-Jones, isn't he the chap you all suspected of killing Fraser?" asked Bishop.

Schoenbeck looked pained. "Unfortunately, yes. Of all the guests at the clinic he persisted in remaining a mystery. It appears that the man is nothing less than a jewel thief."

Mrs. Pollifax said calmly, "Yes, and a very *good* jewel thief. I'm delighted he's told you about himself but you must see that by being honest with you he's completely ruined his career." She looked at Schoenbeck sternly. "Is there anything you care to do about that M. Schoenbeck?"

His glance moved to hers and he smiled faintly. "Yes, madame, there is, but I am wondering how you guessed it."

"It's an idea that frankly occurred to me several days

ago," she said. "Perhaps you're reading my mind, M. Schoenbeck."

"Mon Dieu, one hopes not!"

"He's tremendously efficient about picking locks and he enjoys working alone, he's surprisingly clever in emergencies and he has gorgeous clothes."

Schoenbeck said dryly, "The clothes would do it, of course. As a matter of fact, madame, I am not such a fool as to allow such talent to slip through my fingers. I have already made certain approaches and he appears most interested." He added ruefully. "I can only wish that young Hafez could work for Interpol, too. Now there's a promising young brain."

"I think he prefers to become an astronomer," put in Mrs. Pollifax. "Where is he?"

"He and his grandmother are still talking to his father on the telephone, I believe, but he is anxious to see you when I have finished with you."

She shook her head in wonder. "It's incredible how resourceful he's been. If it hadn't been for Hafez—"

"Please," Schoenbeck said firmly. "Please, it is better, as you say, to have no post-mortems. Allow me instead to conduct them and to brood over how near Kashan came to pulling off his coup and completing his matched set of plutonium."

"What will happen to him?" she asked.

Schoenbeck sighed. "Very little, I fear. It is an unfortunate fact but—so far as I can see—no crime has been committed by the sheik except that of conspiracy, and this King Jarroud will have to deal with on a local level. The sheik paid others to kill for him, and it is they who will be punished. It is a pity but I think he will suffer only a little embarrassment and—one hopes—a few grave doubts that Allah personally spoke to him."

"Even when he planned to threaten the world with an atom bomb?" protested Mrs. Pollifax. "He said he had an army in the desert, and laboratories—and obviously he had a network of people available to him if he succeeded in stealing plutonium."

"We can only hope, madame," said Schoenbeck, "but we have discovered that before he left Switzerland the sheik had time to make a telephone call to Zabya. I fear that we may find only empty laboratories—if we find them at all—and as for a secret army I suspect the sheik has already ordered it disbanded or moved."

"Moved!" cried Mrs. Pollifax in a dismayed voice.

"Naturally he will not dare to try his *coup d'etat* tomorrow but he still has several pounds of plutonium, madame. Dreams die hard."

"Oh dear," said Mrs. Pollifax.

He nodded. "I am not overly optimistic that Kashan's ambitions have been deflated. I can assure you that the sheik will be closely watched but I must tell you that the desert is enormous, madame, and much of it uncharted." He sighed. "When I grow depressed—as one does—about the frailties of civilization and the absence of saints, it is men like the sheik who give me patience. A number of governments muddling along give us a thin margin of error but it is nevertheless a margin against oblivion."

She said reluctantly, "He impressed me, you know."

Schoenbeck smiled. "But of course, Madame—the sheik would make the perfect anti-Christ."

"I beg your pardon?" said Bishop, startled.

Schoenbeck's mouth twisted humorously. "You do not know your Bible? It is prophesied that after the Jews regain Jerusalem—as they did several years ago—there will come the anti-Christ, a man who will perform miracles for the people and bring peace to the world. And—how does it go?" His eyes narrowed thoughtfully. " 'And when the people shall say—peace and safety!—then suddenly destruction will come upon them as travail upon a woman with child, and they shall not escape.' Thessalonians, I believe." He bowed to them and strolled toward the door.

"Monsieur Schoenbeck," Mrs. Pollifax called after him

softly. "The plutonium is in the basement supply room, in the farthest corner hidden behind a sack of charcoal."

He smiled. "Thank you, madame."

"Odd duck," said Bishop when he had gone. "On the whole, I believe Carstairs was a bit rough on him." He, too, arose. "Well, Mrs. Pollifax," he said, walking over to kiss her lightly on the cheek, "it's time for me to fly away again. You've orders to stay through the week until you've thoroughly convalesced, you know. If you don't, Carstairs will have my head for it."

"But I'm delighted to stay," said Mrs. Pollifax, "and actually quite relieved that I may. Can you imagine Miss Hartshorne's reaction if I should go back to New Brunswick with my arm like this?" She shook her head at the thought. "She'll be very difficult, at least until Christmas. She'll say it's exactly what I deserve for spending a dull week in Baltimore visiting an old friend." With a small twinkle she added, "Miss Hartshorne feels I lack a sense of adventure."

"Good God," said Bishop with a shudder. "And if you're still in a sling when you go home what will you tell her?"

"That I tripped over Adelaide's cat, I think, and broke my arm."

"A very large cat?" suggested Bishop, grinning.

"Oh, very," she told him, smiling.

"Then I needn't worry about you any more. By the way, I think you'll find yourself in good company this week. Hafez and his grandmother will be staying a few days until Madame Parviz feels better. General Parviz will fly over on Friday to take them home and I imagine the general will be eager to meet you."

From the door Hafez said, "Please, may we come in now, monsieur?"

"She's all yours," Bishop said, and blowing Mrs. Pollifax a kiss went out.

Hafez, Robin, and Court tiptoed in and stood at the end

of the bed beaming at her while she in turn beamed at them. She saw that Robin and Court were holding hands and she guessed that Robin, having unburdened himself to Interpol, had unburdened himself to Court as well. Mrs. Pollifax said mischievously, *"Ici la police. Sortez, les mains en l'air!"*

Hafez broke into a laugh and hurled himself across the bed to sit near her, his face shining with happiness. "Madame," he said, "we are all alive."

"Isn't it surprising?" she agreed.

"And, madame," he continued eagerly, "I have been speaking to my father on the telephone—twice we have talked—and you will meet him on Friday because they say you cannot travel yet, and he wishes to thank you in person and—"

"Hafez is back to normal," pointed out Robin, grinning.

"—and he is bringing from King Jarroud the Shepherd Isa Medal of Peace—"

"Shepherd Medal?" asked Court, sitting down.

"Yes, mademoiselle, named after the shepherd Isa, who saved our country from invasion in 1236. He threw himself from a cliff to warn the people in the valley that the enemy was on the hills, and when they saw his fall, with the enemy's arrow piercing his heart, they knew their country was in danger. And my father says on Friday we will have a small party here at the Clinic to present to you this medal, the highest given in my country. Isn't that magnificent, madame?"

"And you didn't even have to throw yourself off a cliff," pointed out Robin.

Court shivered. "You have all—the three of you—been in such danger and I didn't even know. I didn't *know.*"

Hafez turned and looked at her and was glad to hear the sadness in her voice.

Robin, too, turned to look at Court. "If I'm going to work for Interpol—now that Mrs. Pollifax has succeeded in making an honest man of me—you'll have to grow accustomed to a spot or two of danger, you know. That is, if you're going to marry me."

Court said softly, *"Am* I going to marry you, Robin?"

"I'm damned well hoping so."

Her cheeks turned pink. "Well," she said thoughtfully, and then, "Yes . . . I believe I am!" she said in astonishment.

"Bravo," said Mrs. Pollifax.

Robin leaned down and kissed the top of Court's dark head. "The wisest decision you've ever made, my dear, and it gives me a perfectly brilliant idea. If Hafez's party is Friday it gives us just time to get a special license. We can be married right here at the Clinic."

"And Mrs. Pollifax can be the matron of honor," cried Court. "Oh you simply must be my matron of honor, Mrs. Pollifax. You will, won't you?"

Mrs. Pollifax considered this with pleasure. "I can't think of anything I'd enjoy more," she confessed. "I can wear my drip-dry purple robe and my prayer beads. It's been *such* a disappointment that I've been too busy to wear either of them."

"That I can't wait to see," Robin said fervently.

"But who could be the best man?"

"Oh, no problem there," Robin said, and placed a hand on Hafez's shoulder. "There's only one person at the Clinic or anywhere else who could possibly qualify."

Hafez looked up at Robin and grinned.

With a blissful sigh Mrs. Pollifax leaned back against her pillows to watch them. She acknowledged that her arm was stiff and uncomfortable, and that ahead of her lay the greatest ordeal of all—Miss Hartshorne—but what is brought by the wind, she remembered, will be carried away by the wind. With this she dismissed all thoughts of the sheik and settled down to enjoy a really genuine convalescence.